Dover Thrift Study Edition

Much Ado About Nothing

WILLIAM SHAKESPEARE

DOVER PUBLICATIONS, INC.
Mineola, New York

Bibliographical Note

This Dover edition, first published in 2010, contains the unabridged text of *Much Ado About Nothing,* as it appeared in Volume II of the second edition of *The Works of William Shakespeare,* published by Macmillan and Co., London, 1891, plus literary analysis and perspectives from *MAXnotes® for Much Ado About Nothing,* published in 1996 by Research and Education Association, Inc., Piscataway, New Jersey. The explanatory footnotes to the play have been supplemented and revised from the Macmillan edition.

International Standard Book Number

ISBN-13: 978-0-486-47579-0
ISBN-10: 0-486-47579-4

Manufactured in the United States by Courier Corporation
47579402
www.doverpublications.com

Publisher's Note

Combining the complete text of a classic novel or drama with a comprehensive study guide, Dover Thrift Study Editions are the most effective way to gain a thorough understanding of the major works of world literature.

The study guide features up-to-date and expert analysis of every chapter or section from the source work. Questions and fully explained answers follow, allowing readers to analyze the material critically. Character lists, author bios, and discussions of the work's historical context are also provided.

Each Dover Thrift Study Edition includes everything a student needs to prepare for homework, discussions, reports, and exams.

Contents

Much Ado About Nothing

WILLIAM SHAKESPEARE

Contents

Dramatis Personæ

DON PEDRO, prince of Arragon.
DON JOHN, his bastard brother.
CLAUDIO, a young lord of Florence.
BENEDICK, a young lord of Padua.
LEONATO, governor of Messina.
ANTONIO, his brother.
BALTHASAR, attendant on Don Pedro.
CONRADE, } followers of Don John.
BORACHIO, }
FRIAR FRANCIS.
DOGBERRY, a constable.
VERGES, a headborough.[1]
A Sexton.
A Boy.

HERO, daughter to Leonato.
BEATRICE, niece to Leonato.
Margaret, } gentlewomen attending on Hero.
Ursula, }

Messengers, Watch, Attendants, &c.

Scene — *Messina.*

---

1. *headborough*] a kind of village-mayor.

ACT I.

SCENE I. *Before* LEONATO'S *house*.

Enter LEONATO, HERO, *and* BEATRICE, *with a* Messenger.

LEON. I learn in this letter that Don Pedro of Arragon comes this night to Messina.

MESS. He is very near by this: he was not three leagues off when I left him.

LEON. How many gentlemen have you lost in this action?

MESS. But few of any sort, and none of name.

LEON. A victory is twice itself when the achiever brings home full numbers. I find here that Don Pedro hath bestowed much honour on a young Florentine called Claudio.

MESS. Much deserved on his part, and equally remembered by Don Pedro: he hath borne himself beyond the promise of his age; doing, in the figure of a lamb, the feats of a lion: he hath indeed better bettered expectation than you must expect of me to tell you how.

LEON. He hath an uncle here in Messina will be very much glad of it.

MESS. I have already delivered him letters, and there appears much joy in him; even so much, that joy could not show itself modest enough without a badge of bitterness.

LEON. Did he break out into tears?

MESS. In great measure.

LEON. A kind overflow of kindness: there are no faces truer than those that are so washed. How much better is it to weep at joy than to joy at weeping!

BEAT. I pray you, is Signior Mountanto[1] returned from the wars or no?

---

1. *Mountanto*] a fencing term for an upward thrust.

1

MESS.   I know none of that name, lady: there was none such in the army of any sort.

LEON.   What is he that you ask for, niece?

HERO.   My cousin means Signior Benedick of Padua.

MESS.   O, he's returned; and as pleasant as ever he was.

BEAT.   He set up his bills here in Messina and challenged Cupid at the flight;[2] and my uncle's fool, reading the challenge, subscribed for Cupid, and challenged him at the bird-bolt.[3] I pray you, how many hath he killed and eaten in these wars? But how many hath he killed? for, indeed, I promised to eat all of his killing.

LEON.   Faith, niece, you tax Signior Benedick too much; but he'll be meet with you, I doubt it not.

MESS.   He hath done good service, lady, in these wars.

BEAT.   You had musty victual, and he hath holp to eat it: he is a very valiant trencher-man;[4] he hath an excellent stomach.

MESS.   And a good soldier too, lady.

BEAT.   And a good soldier to a lady; but what is he to a lord?

MESS.   A lord to a lord, a man to a man; stuffed with all honourable virtues.

BEAT.   It is so, indeed; he is no less than a stuffed man: but for the stuffing,—well, we are all mortal.

LEON.   You must not, sir, mistake my niece. There is a kind of merry war betwixt Signior Benedick and her: they never meet but there's a skirmish of wit between them.

BEAT.   Alas! he gets nothing by that. In our last conflict four of his five wits[5] went halting off, and now is the whole man governed with one: so that if he have wit enough to keep himself warm, let him bear it for a difference between himself and his horse; for it is all the wealth that he hath left, to be known a reasonable creature. Who is his companion now? He hath every month a new sworn brother.

MESS.   Is't possible?

---

2. *flight*] long-distance shooting.

3. *bird-bolt*] a short, blunt, stumpy arrow used for killing birds.

4. *trencher-man*] a trencher is a plate; Beatrice is making fun of Benedick's appetite.

5. *five wits*] distinguished from the five senses, the five wits were common wit, imagination, fantasy, judgment and memory.

BEAT.   Very easily possible: he wears his faith but as the fashion of his
hat; it ever changes with the next block.

MESS.   I see, lady, the gentleman is not in your books.

BEAT.   No; an he were, I would burn my study. But, I pray you, who is
his companion? Is there no young squarer⁶ now that will make a
voyage with him to the devil?

MESS.   He is most in the company of the right noble Claudio.

BEAT.   O Lord, he will hang upon him like a disease: he is sooner
caught than the pestilence, and the taker runs presently mad. God
help the noble Claudio! if he have caught the Benedick, it will cost
him a thousand pound ere a' be cured.

MESS.   I will hold friends with you, lady.

BEAT.   Do, good friend.

LEON.   You will never run mad, niece.

BEAT.   No, not till a hot January.

MESS.   Don Pedro is approached.

Enter DON PEDRO, DON JOHN, CLAUDIO, BENEDICK, *and* BALTHASAR.

D. PEDRO.   Good Signior Leonato, you are come to meet your trouble:
the fashion of the world is to avoid cost, and you encounter it.

LEON.   Never came trouble to my house in the likeness of your Grace:
for trouble being gone, comfort should remain; but when you
depart from me, sorrow abides, and happiness takes his leave.

D. PEDRO.   You embrace your charge too willingly. I think this is your
daughter.

LEON.   Her mother hath many times told me so.

BENE.   Were you in doubt, sir, that you asked her?

LEON.   Signior Benedick, no; for then were you a child.

D. PEDRO.   You have it full, Benedick: we may guess by this what you
are, being a man. Truly, the lady fathers herself. Be happy, lady; for
you are like an honourable father.

BENE.   If Signior Leonato be her father, she would not have his head
on her shoulders for all Messina, as like him as she is.

BEAT.   I wonder that you will still be talking, Signior Benedick: nobody
marks you.

_____

6. *squarer*] braggart.

BENE. What, my dear Lady Disdain! are you yet living?

BEAT. Is it possible disdain should die while she hath such meet food to feed it, as Signior Benedick? Courtesy itself must convert to disdain, if you come in her presence.

BENE. Then is courtesy a turncoat. But it is certain I am loved of all ladies, only you excepted: and I would I could find in my heart that I had not a hard heart; for, truly, I love none.

BEAT. A dear happiness to women: they would else have been troubled with a pernicious suitor. I thank God and my cold blood, I am of your humour for that: I had rather hear my dog bark at a crow than a man swear he loves me.

BENE. God keep your ladyship still in that mind! so some gentleman or other shall 'scape a predestinate scratched face.

BEAT. Scratching could not make it worse, an 'twere such a face as yours were.

BENE. Well, you are a rare parrot-teacher.

BEAT. A bird of my tongue is better than a beast of yours.

BENE. I would my horse had the speed of your tongue, and so good a continuer. But keep your way, i' God's name; I have done.

BEAT. You always end with a jade's trick: I know you of old.

D. PEDRO. That is the sum of all, Leonato. Signior Claudio and Signior Benedick, my dear friend Leonato hath invited you all. I tell him we shall stay here at the least a month; and he heartily prays some occasion may detain us longer. I dare swear he is no hypocrite, but prays from his heart.

LEON. If you swear, my lord, you shall not be forsworn. [*To* DON JOHN] Let me bid you welcome, my lord: being reconciled to the prince your brother, I owe you all duty.

D. JOHN. I thank you: I am not of many words, but I thank you.

LEON. Please it your Grace lead on?

D. PEDRO. Your hand, Leonato; we will go together.

[*Exeunt all except* BENEDICK *and* CLAUDIO.]

CLAUD. Benedick, didst thou note the daughter of Signior Leonato?

BENE. I noted her not; but I looked on her.

CLAUD. Is she not a modest young lady?

BENE. Do you question me, as an honest man should do, for my simple true judgement? or would you have me speak after my custom, as being a professed tyrant to their sex?

CLAUD. No; I pray thee speak in sober judgement.

BENE. Why, i'faith, methinks she's too low for a high praise, too
   brown for a fair praise, and too little for a great praise: only this
   commendation I can afford her, that were she other than she is,
   she were unhandsome; and being no other but as she is, I do not
   like her.

CLAUD. Thou thinkest I am in sport: I pray thee tell me truly how thou
   likest her.

BENE. Would you buy her, that you inquire after her?

CLAUD. Can the world buy such a jewel?

BENE. Yea, and a case to put it into. But speak you this with a sad
   brow? or do you play the flouting Jack, to tell us Cupid is a good
   hare-finder,[7] and Vulcan a rare carpenter? Come, in what key shall
   a man take you, to go in the song?

CLAUD. In mine eye she is the sweetest lady that ever I looked on.

BENE. I can see yet without spectacles, and I see no such matter:
   there's her cousin, an she were not possessed with a fury, exceeds
   her as much in beauty as the first of May doth the last of December.
   But I hope you have no intent to turn husband, have you?

CLAUD. I would scarce trust myself, though I had sworn the contrary,
   if Hero would be my wife.

BENE. Is't come to this? In faith, hath not the world one man but he
   will wear his cap with suspicion? Shall I never see a bachelor of
   threescore again? Go to, i'faith; an thou wilt needs thrust thy neck
   into a yoke, wear the print of it, and sigh away Sundays. Look; Don
   Pedro is returned to seek you.

Re-enter DON PEDRO.

D. PEDRO. What secret hath held you here, that you followed not to
   Leonato's?

BENE. I would your Grace would constrain me to tell.

D. PEDRO. I charge thee on thy allegiance.

BENE. You hear, Count Claudio: I can be secret as a dumb man; I
   would have you think so; but, on my allegiance, mark you this, on
   my allegiance. He is in love. With who? now that is your Grace's
   part. Mark how short his answer is;—With Hero, Leonato's short
   daughter.

---

7. *hare-finder*] a director of a hare hunt, chosen for his keen vision.

CLAUD. If this were so, so were it uttered.

BENE. Like the old tale, my lord: 'it is not so, nor 'twas not so, but, indeed, God forbid it should be so.'

CLAUD. If my passion change not shortly, God forbid it should be otherwise.

D. PEDRO. Amen, if you love her; for the lady is very well worthy.

CLAUD. You speak this to fetch me in, my lord.

D. PEDRO. By my troth, I speak my thought.

CLAUD. And, in faith, my lord, I spoke mine.

BENE. And, by my two faiths and troths, my lord, I spoke mine.

CLAUD. That I love her, I feel.

D. PEDRO. That she is worthy, I know.

BENE. That I neither feel how she should be loved, nor know how she should be worthy, is the opinion that fire cannot melt out of me: I will die in it at the stake.

D. PEDRO. Thou wast ever an obstinate heretic in the despite of beauty.

CLAUD. And never could maintain his part but in the force of his will.

BENE. That a woman conceived me, I thank her; that she brought me up, I likewise give her most humble thanks: but that I will have a recheat winded in my forehead,[8] or hang my bugle in an invisible baldrick,[9] all women shall pardon me. Because I will not do them the wrong to mistrust any, I will do myself the right to trust none; and the fine is, for the which I may go the finer, I will live a bachelor.

D. PEDRO. I shall see thee, ere I die, look pale with love.

BENE. With anger, with sickness, or with hunger, my lord; not with love: prove that ever I lose more blood with love than I will get again with drinking, pick out mine eyes with a ballad-maker's pen, and hang me up at the door of a brothel-house for the sign of blind Cupid.

D. PEDRO. Well, if ever thou dost fall from this faith, thou wilt prove a notable argument.

---

8. *a recheat . . . forehead*] to "wind a recheat" is to sound a note on the huntsman's bugle; Benedick refers to the popular notion that horns sprout from the forehead of a cuckolded husband.

9. *baldrick*] the belt in which the huntsman's bugle is carried.

BENE.   If I do, hang me in a bottle like a cat, and shoot at me; and he that hits me, let him be clapped on the shoulder and called Adam.[10]

D. PEDRO.   Well, as time shall try:
'In time the savage bull doth bear the yoke.'

BENE.   The savage bull may; but if ever the sensible Benedick bear it, pluck off the bull's horns, and set them in my forehead: and let me be vilely painted; and in such great letters as they write 'Here is good horse to hire,' let them signify under my sign 'Here you may see Benedick the married man.'

CLAUD.   If this should ever happen, thou wouldst be horn-mad.

D. PEDRO.   Nay, if Cupid have not spent all his quiver in Venice, thou wilt quake for this shortly.

BENE.   I look for an earthquake too, then.

D. PEDRO.   Well, you will temporize with the hours. In the meantime, good Signior Benedick, repair to Leonato's: commend me to him, and tell him I will not fail him at supper; for indeed he hath made great preparation.

BENE.   I have almost matter enough in me for such an embassage; and so I commit you —

CLAUD.   To the tuition of God: From my house, if I had it, —

D. PEDRO.   The sixth of July:[11] Your loving friend, Benedick.

BENE.   Nay, mock not, mock not. The body of your discourse is sometime guarded with fragments, and the guards are but slightly basted on neither: ere you flout old ends any further, examine your conscience: and so I leave you.   [Exit.]

CLAUD.   My liege, your highness now may do me good.

D. PEDRO.   My love is thine to teach: teach it but how,
And thou shalt see how apt it is to learn
Any hard lesson that may do thee good.

CLAUD.   Hath Leonato any son, my lord?

D. PEDRO.   No child but Hero; she's his only heir.

---

10. *hang me ... Adam*] shooting at a cat enclosed in a wooden bottle or barrel was a favorite country sport; "Adam" may be a reference to Adam Bell, the outlaw of ballad tradition, held to be a champion archer.

11. *The sixth of July*] Midsummer-day according to older calculations; a fit date for midsummer madness.

Dost thou affect her, Claudio?

CLAUD.   O, my lord,
When you went onward on this ended action,
I look'd upon her with a soldier's eye,
That liked, but had a rougher task in hand
Than to drive liking to the name of love:
But now I am return'd and that war-thoughts
Have left their places vacant, in their rooms
Come thronging soft and delicate desires,
All prompting me how fair young Hero is,
Saying, I liked her ere I went to wars.

D. PEDRO.   Thou wilt be like a lover presently,
And tire the hearer with a book of words.
If thou dost love fair Hero, cherish it;
And I will break[12] with her and with her father,
And thou shalt have her. Was't not to this end
That thou began'st to twist so fine a story?

CLAUD.   How sweetly you do minister to love,
That know love's grief by his complexion!
But lest my liking might too sudden seem,
I would have salved it with a longer treatise.

D. PEDRO.   What need the bridge much broader than the flood?
The fairest grant is the necessity.
Look, what will serve is fit: 'tis once, thou lovest,
And I will fit thee with the remedy.
I know we shall have revelling to-night:
I will assume thy part in some disguise,
And tell fair Hero I am Claudio;
And in her bosom I'll unclasp my heart,
And take her hearing prisoner with the force
And strong encounter of my amorous tale:
Then after to her father will I break;
And the conclusion is, she shall be thine.
In practice let us put it presently.   [*Exeunt.*]

---

12. *break*] broach (the subject).

SCENE II. *A room in* LEONATO'S *house*.

Enter LEONATO *and* ANTONIO, *meeting*.

LEON.   How now, brother! Where is my cousin, your son? hath he
provided this music?

ANT.   He is very busy about it. But, brother, I can tell you strange news,
that you yet dreamt not of.

LEON.   Are they good?

ANT.   As the event stamps them: but they have a good cover; they show
well outward. The prince and Count Claudio, walking in a thick-
pleached[1] alley in mine orchard, were thus much overheard by a
man of mine: the prince discovered[2] to Claudio that he loved my
niece your daughter, and meant to acknowledge it this night in a
dance; and if he found her accordant, he meant to take the present
time by the top, and instantly break with you of it.

LEON.   Hath the fellow any wit that told you this?

ANT.   A good sharp fellow: I will send for him; and question him
yourself.

LEON.   No, no; we will hold it as a dream till it appear itself: but I will
acquaint my daughter withal, that she may be the better prepared
for an answer, if peradventure this be true. Go you and tell her of it.
[*Enter* Attendants.] Cousins, you know what you have to do. O, I
cry you mercy, friend; go you with me, and I will use your skill.
Good cousin, have a care this busy time.   [*Exeunt.*]

---

1. *thick-pleached*] with boughs thickly plaited or intertwined.
2. *discovered*] revealed.

SCENE III. *The same*.

Enter DON JOHN *and* CONRADE.

CON. What the good-year, my lord! why are you thus out of measure
    sad?

D. JOHN. There is no measure in the occasion that breeds; therefore
    the sadness is without limit.

CON. You should hear reason.

D. JOHN. And when I have heard it, what blessing brings it?

CON. If not a present remedy, at least a patient sufferance.

D. JOHN. I wonder that thou, being (as thou sayest thou art) born under
    Saturn,[1] goest about to apply a moral medicine to a mortifying
    mischief. I cannot hide what I am: I must be sad when I have cause,
    and smile at no man's jests; eat when I have stomach, and wait for no
    man's leisure; sleep when I am drowsy, and tend on no man's
    business; laugh when I am merry, and claw no man in his humour.

CON. Yea, but you must not make the full show of this till you may do
    it without controlment. You have of late stood out against your
    brother, and he hath ta'en you newly into his grace; where it is
    impossible you should take true root but by the fair weather that
    you make yourself: it is needful that you frame the season for your
    own harvest.

D. JOHN. I had rather be a canker in a hedge than a rose in his grace;
    and it better fits my blood to be disdained of all than to fashion a
    carriage to rob love from any: in this, though I cannot be said to be
    a flattering honest man, it must not be denied but I am a plain-
    dealing villain. I am trusted with a muzzle, and enfranchised with a
    clog;[2] therefore I have decreed not to sing in my cage. If I had my

---

1. *born under Saturn*] of Saturnine or melancholy temperament.
2. *enfranchised with a clog*] set at liberty, but with a "clog" (anything hung upon an animal
    to hinder motion).

mouth, I would bite; if I had my liberty, I would do my liking: in the
meantime let me be that I am, and seek not to alter me.

CON.   Can you make no use of your discontent?

D. JOHN.   I make all use of it, for I use it only.
Who comes here?

Enter BORACHIO.

What news, Borachio?

BORA.   I came yonder from a great supper: the prince your brother is
royally entertained by Leonato; and I can give you intelligence of
an intended marriage.

D. JOHN.   Will it serve for any model to build mischief on? What is he
for a fool that betroths himself to unquietness?

BORA.   Marry, it is your brother's right hand.

D. JOHN.   Who? the most exquisite Claudio?

BORA.   Even he.

D. JOHN.   A proper squire! And who, and who? which way looks he?

BORA.   Marry, on Hero, the daughter and heir of Leonato.

D. JOHN.   A very forward March-chick! How came you to this?

BORA.   Being entertained for a perfumer,[3] as I was smoking a musty
room, comes me the prince and Claudio, hand in hand, in sad
conference: I whipt me behind the arras; and there heard it agreed
upon, that the prince should woo Hero for himself, and having
obtained her, give her to Count Claudio.

D. JOHN.   Come, come, let us thither: this may prove food to my
displeasure. That young start-up hath all the glory of my overthrow:
if I can cross him any way, I bless myself every way. You are both
sure, and will assist me?

CON.   To the death, my lord.

D. JOHN.   Let us to the great supper: their cheer is the greater that I am
subdued. Would the cook were of my mind! Shall we go prove
what's to be done?

BORA.   We'll wait upon your lordship.   [*Exeunt.*]

---

3. *entertained . . . perfumer*] Borachio is mistaken for someone who perfumes rooms by
smoking aromatic herbs in a censer.

ACT II.

Scene I. A *hall in* Leonato's *house*.

Enter Leonato, Antonio, Hero, Beatrice, *and others*.

Leon. Was not Count John here at supper?

Ant. I saw him not.

Beat. How tartly that gentleman looks! I never can see him but I am heart-burned an hour after.

Hero. He is of a very melancholy disposition.

Beat. He were an excellent man that were made just in the midway between him and Benedick: the one is too like an image and says nothing, and the other too like my lady's eldest son, evermore tattling.

Leon. Then half Signior Benedick's tongue in Count John's mouth, and half Count John's melancholy in Signior Benedick's face,—

Beat. With a good leg and a good foot, uncle, and money enough in his purse, such a man would win any woman in the world, if a' could get her good-will.

Leon. By my troth, niece, thou wilt never get thee a husband, if thou be so shrewd[1] of thy tongue.

Ant. In faith, she's too curst.

Beat. Too curst is more than curst: I shall lessen God's sending that way; for it is said, 'God sends a curst cow short horns;' but to a cow too curst he sends none.

Leon. So, by being too curst, God will send you no horns.

Beat. Just, if he send me no husband; for the which blessing I am at

---

1. *shrewd*] vicious, bad-tempered.

him upon my knees every morning and evening. Lord, I could not endure a husband with a beard on his face: I had rather lie in the woollen.[2]

LEON. You may light on a husband that hath no beard.

BEAT. What should I do with him? dress him in my apparel, and make him my waiting-gentlewoman? He that hath a beard is more than a youth; and he that hath no beard is less than a man: and he that is more than a youth is not for me; and he that is less than a man, I am not for him: therefore I will even take sixpence in earnest of the bear-ward, and lead his apes into hell.

LEON. Well, then, go you into hell?

BEAT. No, but to the gate; and there will the devil meet me, like an old cuckold, with horns on his head, and say 'Get you to heaven, Beatrice, get you to heaven; here's no place for you maids:' so deliver I up my apes, and away to Saint Peter for the heavens; he shows me where the bachelors sit, and there live we as merry as the day is long.

ANT. [*To Hero*] Well, niece, I trust you will be ruled by your father.

BEAT. Yes, faith; it is my cousin's duty to make courtesy, and say, 'Father, as it please you.' But yet for all that, cousin, let him be a handsome fellow, or else make another courtesy, and say, 'Father, as it please me.'

LEON. Well, niece, I hope to see you one day fitted with a husband.

BEAT. Not till God make men of some other metal than earth. Would it not grieve a woman to be overmastered with a piece of valiant dust? to make an account of her life to a clod of wayward marl? No, uncle, I'll none: Adam's sons are my brethren; and, truly, I hold it a sin to match in my kindred.

LEON. Daughter, remember what I told you: if the prince do solicit you in that kind, you know your answer.

BEAT. The fault will be in the music, cousin, if you be not wooed in good time: if the prince be too important, tell him there is measure in every thing, and so dance out the answer. For, hear me, Hero: wooing, wedding, and repenting, is as a Scotch jig, a measure, and

---

2. *woollen*] shroud.

a cinque pace:[3] the first suit is hot and hasty, like a Scotch jig, and full as fantastical; the wedding, mannerly-modest, as a measure, full of state and ancientry; and then comes repentance, and, with his bad legs, falls into the cinque pace faster and faster, till he sink into his grave.

LEON. Cousin, you apprehend passing shrewdly.

BEAT. I have a good eye, uncle; I can see a church by daylight.

LEON. The revellers are entering, brother: make good room.

[*All put on their masks.*]

Enter DON PEDRO, CLAUDIO, BENEDICK, BALTHASAR, DON JOHN, BORACHIO, MARGARET, URSULA, *and others, masked.*

D. PEDRO. Lady, will you walk about with your friend?

HERO. So you walk softly, and look sweetly, and say nothing, I am yours for the walk; and especially when I walk away.

D. PEDRO. With me in your company?

HERO. I may say so, when I please.

D. PEDRO. And when please you to say so?

HERO. When I like your favour; for God defend the lute should be like the case!

D. PEDRO. My visor is Philemon's roof; within the house is Jove.

HERO. Why, then, your visor should be thatched.[4]

D. PEDRO. Speak low, if you speak love.   [*Drawing her aside.*]

BALTH. Well, I would you did like me.

MARG. So would not I, for your own sake; for I have many ill qualities.

BALTH. Which is one?

MARG. I say my prayers aloud.

BALTH. I love you the better: the hearers may cry, Amen.

MARG. God match me with a good dancer!

BALTH. Amen.

MARG. And God keep him out of my sight when the dance is done! Answer, clerk.

---

3. *cinque pace*] the French dance called "cinq pas" or "galliard," of which each complete movement consisted of five steps; the pace quickened as the dance continued. The word is often written "sink-a-pace."

4. *Philemon's roof . . . thatched*] In Ovid's *Metamorphoses* (VIII, 630), two peasants, Philemon and Baucis, unknowingly entertained Jove and Mercury in their rustic thatch-roofed cottage.

BALTH. No more words: the clerk is answered.

URS. I know you well enough; you are Signior Antonio.

ANT. At a word, I am not.

URS. I know you by the waggling of your head.

ANT. To tell you true, I counterfeit him.

URS. You could never do him so ill-well, unless you were the very man. Here's his dry hand up and down: you are he, you are he.

ANT. At a word, I am not.

URS. Come, come, do you think I do not know you by your excellent wit? can virtue hide itself? Go to, mum, you are he: graces will appear, and there's an end.

BEAT. Will you not tell me who told you so?

BENE. No, you shall pardon me.

BEAT. Nor will you not tell me who you are?

BENE. Not now.

BEAT. That I was disdainful, and that I had my good wit out of the 'Hundred Merry Tales':[5]—well, this was Signior Benedick that said so.

BENE. What's he?

BEAT. I am sure you know him well enough.

BENE. Not I, believe me.

BEAT. Did he never make you laugh?

BENE. I pray you, what is he?

BEAT. Why, he is the prince's jester: a very dull fool; only his gift is in devising impossible slanders: none but libertines delight in him; and the commendation is not in his wit, but in his villany; for he both pleases men and angers them, and then they laugh at him and beat him. I am sure he is in the fleet: I would he had boarded me.

BENE. When I know the gentleman, I'll tell him what you say.

BEAT. Do, do: he'll but break a comparison or two on me; which, peradventure not marked or not laughed at, strikes him into melancholy; and then there's a partridge wing saved, for the fool will eat no supper that night. [*Music.*] We must follow the leaders.

BENE. In every good thing.

BEAT. Nay, if they lead to any ill, I will leave them at the next turning.

---

5. '*Hundred Merry Tales*'] the title of a popular joke book, first published in 1526 and frequently reissued.

[*Dance. Then exeunt all except* DON JOHN, BORACHIO, *and* CLAUDIO.]

D. JOHN.   Sure my brother is amorous on Hero, and hath withdrawn her father to break with him about it. The ladies follow her, and but one visor remains.

BORA.   And that is Claudio: I know him by his bearing.

D. JOHN.   Are not you Signior Benedick?

CLAUD.   You know me well; I am he.

D. JOHN.   Signior, you are very near my brother in his love: he is enamoured on Hero; I pray you, dissuade him from her: she is no equal for his birth: you may do the part of an honest man in it.

CLAUD.   How know you he loves her?

D. JOHN.   I heard him swear his affection.

BORA.   So did I too; and he swore he would marry her to-night.

D. JOHN.   Come, let us to the banquet.

                        [*Exeunt* DON JOHN *and* BORACHIO.]

CLAUD.   Thus answer I in name of Benedick,
But hear these ill news with the ears of Claudio.
'Tis certain so; the prince wooes for himself.
Friendship is constant in all other things
Save in the office and affairs of love:
Therefore all hearts in love use their own tongues;
Let every eye negotiate for itself,
And trust no agent; for beauty is a witch,
Against whose charms faith melteth into blood.
This is an accident of hourly proof,
Which I mistrusted not. Farewell, therefore, Hero!

Re-enter BENEDICK.

BENE.   Count Claudio?

CLAUD.   Yea, the same.

BENE.   Come, will you go with me?

CLAUD.   Whither?

BENE.   Even to the next willow, about your own business, county. What fashion will you wear the garland of? about your neck, like an usurer's chain? or under your arm, like a lieutenant's scarf? You must wear it one way, for the prince hath got your Hero.

CLAUD.   I wish him joy of her.

BENE. Why, that's spoken like an honest drovier;[6] so they sell bullocks. But did you think the prince would have served you thus?

CLAUD. I pray you, leave me.

BENE. Ho! now you strike like the blind man; 'twas the boy that stole your meat, and you'll beat the post.

CLAUD. If it will not be, I'll leave you. [*Exit*.]

BENE. Alas, poor hurt fowl! now will he creep into sedges. But, that my Lady Beatrice should know me, and not know me! The prince's fool! Ha? It may be I go under that title because I am merry. Yea, but so I am apt to do myself wrong; I am not so reputed: it is the base, though bitter, disposition of Beatrice that puts the world into her person, and so gives me out. Well, I'll be revenged as I may.

Re-enter DON PEDRO.

D. PEDRO. Now, signior, where's the count? did you see him?

BENE. Troth, my lord, I have played the part of Lady Fame. I found him here as melancholy as a lodge in a warren:[7] I told him, and I think I told him true, that your grace had got the good will of this young lady; and I offered him my company to a willow-tree, either to make him a garland, as being forsaken, or to bind him up a rod, as being worthy to be whipped.

D. PEDRO. To be whipped! What's his fault?

BENE. The flat transgression of a school-boy, who, being overjoyed with finding a birds' nest, shows it his companion, and he steals it.

D. PEDRO. Wilt thou make a trust a transgression? The transgression is in the stealer.

BENE. Yet it had not been amiss the rod had been made, and the garland too; for the garland he might have worn himself, and the rod he might have bestowed on you, who, as I take it, have stolen his birds' nest.

D. PEDRO. I will but teach them to sing, and restore them to the owner.

BENE. If their singing answer your saying, by my faith, you say honestly.

---

6. *drovier*] cattle dealer.

7. *a lodge in a warren*] a keeper's hut, necessarily isolated in a game preserve.

D. PEDRO.   The Lady Beatrice hath a quarrel to you: the gentleman
that danced with her told her she is much wronged by you.

BENE.   O, she misused me past the endurance of a block! an oak but
with one green leaf on it would have answered her; my very visor
began to assume life and scold with her. She told me, not thinking I
had been myself, that I was the prince's jester, that I was duller than
a great thaw; huddling jest upon jest, with such impossible convey-
ance, upon me, that I stood like a man at a mark, with a whole army
shooting at me. She speaks poniards, and every word stabs: if her
breath were as terrible as her terminations,[8] there were no living
near her; she would infect to the north star. I would not marry her,
though she were endowed with all that Adam had left him before
he transgressed: she would have made Hercules have turned spit,
yea, and have cleft his club to make the fire too. Come, talk not of
her: you shall find her the infernal Ate[9] in good apparel. I would to
God some scholar would conjure[10] her; for certainly, while she is
here, a man may live as quiet in hell as in a sanctuary; and people
sin upon purpose, because they would go thither; so, indeed, all
disquiet, horror, and perturbation follows her.

D. PEDRO.   Look, here she comes.

Re-enter CLAUDIO, BEATRICE, HERO, *and* LEONATO.

BENE.   Will your grace command me any service to the world's end? I
will go on the slightest errand now to the Antipodes that you can
devise to send me on; I will fetch you a toothpicker now from the
furthest inch of Asia; bring you the length of Prester John's foot;
fetch you a hair off the great Cham's beard; do you any embassage
to the Pigmies;[11] rather than hold three words' conference with this
harpy. You have no employment for me?

D. PEDRO.   None, but to desire your good company.

---

8. *terminations*] terms, epithets.
9. *Ate*] the spirit of discord in Homeric mythology.
10. *conjure*] exorcise; exorcisms were performed in Latin, so the exorcist would have to be a
    scholar.
11. *Prester John's foot . . . Cham's beard . . . Pigmies*] according to romances, Prester John
    was an Asian king of vast wealth; Cham was the supreme ruler of the Mongols; the
    Pigmies were a tribe in the northern mountains of India.

BENE.   O God, sir, here's a dish I love not: I cannot endure my Lady
  Tongue.   [*Exit.*]

D. PEDRO.   Come, lady, come; you have lost the heart of Signior
  Benedick.

BEAT.   Indeed, my lord, he lent it me awhile; and I gave him use for it,
  a double heart for his single one: marry, once before he won it of
  me with false dice, therefore your Grace may well say I have lost it.

D. PEDRO.   You have put him down, lady, you have put him down.

BEAT.   So I would not he should do me, my lord, lest I should prove the
  mother of fools. I have brought Count Claudio, whom you sent me
  to seek.

D. PEDRO.   Why, how now, count! wherefore are you sad?

CLAUD.   Not sad, my lord.

D. PEDRO.   How then? sick?

CLAUD.   Neither, my lord.

BEAT.   The count is neither sad, nor sick, nor merry, nor well; but civil
  count, civil as an orange, and something of that jealous complexion.

D. PEDRO.   I' faith, lady, I think your blazon to be true; though, I'll be
  sworn, if he be so, his conceit is false. Here, Claudio, I have wooed in
  thy name, and fair Hero is won: I have broke with her father, and his
  good will obtained: name the day of marriage, and God give thee joy!

LEON.   Count, take of me my daughter, and with her my fortunes: his
  Grace hath made the match, and all grace say Amen to it.

BEAT.   Speak, count, 'tis your cue.

CLAUD.   Silence is the perfectest herald of joy: I were but little happy,
  if I could say how much. Lady, as you are mine, I am yours: I give
  away myself for you, and dote upon the exchange.

BEAT.   Speak, cousin; or, if you cannot, stop his mouth with a kiss, and
  let not him speak neither.

D. PEDRO.   In faith, lady, you have a merry heart.

BEAT.   Yea, my lord; I thank it, poor fool, it keeps on the windy side of
  care. My cousin tells him in his ear that he is in her heart.

CLAUD.   And so she doth, cousin.

BEAT.   Good Lord, for alliance! Thus goes every one to the world but I,
  and I am sun-burnt;[12] I may sit in a corner, and cry heigh-ho for a
  husband!

---

12. *sun-burnt*] neglected, exposed to the weather, homely, plain.

D. PEDRO.   Lady Beatrice, I will get you one.

BEAT.   I would rather have one of your father's getting. Hath your Grace ne'er a brother like you? Your father got excellent husbands, if a maid could come by them.

D. PEDRO.   Will you have me, lady?

BEAT.   No, my lord, unless I might have another for working-days: your Grace is too costly to wear every day. But, I beseech your Grace, pardon me: I was born to speak all mirth and no matter.

D. PEDRO.   Your silence most offends me, and to be merry best becomes you; for, out of question, you were born in a merry hour.

BEAT.   No, sure, my lord, my mother cried; but then there was a star danced, and under that was I born. Cousins, God give you joy!

LEON.   Niece, will you look to those things I told you of?

BEAT.   I cry you mercy, uncle. By your Grace's pardon.   [Exit.]

D. PEDRO.   By my troth, a pleasant-spirited lady.

LEON.   There's little of the melancholy element in her, my lord: she is never sad but when she sleeps; and not ever sad then; for I have heard my daughter say, she hath often dreamed of unhappiness, and waked herself with laughing.

D. PEDRO.   She cannot endure to hear tell of a husband.

LEON.   O, by no means: she mocks all her wooers out of suit.

D. PEDRO.   She were an excellent wife for Benedick.

LEON.   O Lord, my lord, if they were but a week married, they would talk themselves mad.

D. PEDRO.   County Claudio, when mean you to go to church?

CLAUD.   To-morrow, my lord: time goes on crutches till love have all his rites.

LEON.   Not till Monday, my dear son, which is hence a just sevennight; and a time too brief, too, to have all things answer my mind.

D. PEDRO.   Come, you shake the head at so long a breathing: but, I warrant thee, Claudio, the time shall not go dully by us. I will, in the interim, undertake one of Hercules' labours; which is, to bring Signior Benedick and the Lady Beatrice into a mountain of affection the one with the other. I would fain have it a match; and I doubt not but to fashion it, if you three will but minister such assistance as I shall give you direction.

LEON.   My lord, I am for you, though it cost me ten nights' watchings.

CLAUD.   And I, my lord.

D. PEDRO.   And you too, gentle Hero?

HERO.   I will do any modest office, my lord, to help my cousin to a good husband.

D. PEDRO.   And Benedick is not the unhopefullest husband that I know. Thus far can I praise him; he is of a noble strain, of approved valour, and confirmed honesty. I will teach you how to humour your cousin, that she shall fall in love with Benedick; and I, with your two helps, will so practise on Benedick, that, in despite of his quick wit and his queasy stomach, he shall fall in love with Beatrice. If we can do this, Cupid is no longer an archer: his glory shall be ours, for we are the only love-gods. Go in with me, and I will tell you my drift.   [*Exeunt.*]

SCENE II. *The same.*

Enter DON JOHN *and* BORACHIO.

D. JOHN.   It is so; the Count Claudio shall marry the daughter of Leonato.

BORA.   Yea, my lord; but I can cross it.

D. JOHN.   Any bar, any cross, any impediment will be medicinable to me: I am sick in displeasure to him; and whatsoever comes athwart his affection ranges evenly with mine. How canst thou cross this marriage?

BORA.   Not honestly, my lord; but so covertly that no dishonesty shall appear in me.

D. JOHN.   Show me briefly how.

BORA.   I think I told your lordship, a year since, how much I am in the favour of Margaret, the waiting gentlewoman to Hero.

D. JOHN.   I remember.

BORA.   I can, at any unseasonable instant of the night, appoint her to look out at her lady's chamber window.

D. JOHN.   What life is in that, to be the death of this marriage?

BORA.   The poison of that lies in you to temper. Go you to the prince your brother; spare not to tell him that he hath wronged his honour

in marrying the renowned Claudio—whose estimation do you
mightily hold up—to a contaminated stale, such a one as Hero.

D. JOHN.   What proof shall I make of that?

BORA.   Proof enough to misuse the prince, to vex Claudio, to undo
Hero, and kill Leonato. Look you for any other issue?

D. JOHN.   Only to despite them I will endeavour any thing.

BORA.   Go, then; find me a meet hour to draw Don Pedro and the
Count Claudio alone: tell them that you know that Hero loves me;
intend[1] a kind of zeal both to the prince and Claudio, as,—in love
of your brother's honour, who hath made this match, and his
friend's reputation, who is thus like to be cozened with the semblance of a maid,—that you have discovered thus. They will
scarcely believe this without trial: offer them instances; which shall
bear no less likelihood than to see me at her chamber-window;
hear me call Margaret, Hero; hear Margaret term me Claudio; and
bring them to see this the very night before the intended
wedding,—for in the meantime I will so fashion the matter that
Hero shall be absent,—and there shall appear such seeming truth
of Hero's disloyalty, that jealousy shall be called assurance and all
the preparation overthrown.

D. JOHN.   Grow this to what adverse issue it can, I will put it in
practice. Be cunning in the working this, and thy fee is a thousand
ducats.

BORA.   Be you constant in the accusation, and my cunning shall not
shame me.

D. JOHN.   I will presently go learn their day of marriage.

                                               [*Exeunt.*]

---

1. *intend*] pretend.

SCENE III. LEONATO'S *orchard.*

Enter BENEDICK.

BENE.   Boy!

Enter Boy.

BOY.   Signior?

BENE.   In my chamber-window lies a book: bring it hither to me in the orchard.

BOY.   I am here already, sir.

BENE.   I know that; but I would have thee hence, and here again. [*Exit* Boy.] I do much wonder that one man, seeing how much another man is a fool when he dedicates his behaviours to love, will, after he hath laughed at such shallow follies in others, become the argument of his own scorn by falling in love: and such a man is Claudio. I have known when there was no music with him but the drum and the fife; and now had he rather hear the tabor and the pipe: I have known when he would have walked ten mile a-foot to see a good armour; and now will he lie ten nights awake, carving the fashion of a new doublet. He was wont to speak plain and to the purpose, like an honest man and a soldier; and now is he turned orthography; his words are a very fantastical banquet,—just so many strange dishes. May I be so converted, and see with these eyes? I cannot tell; I think not: I will not be sworn but love may transform me to an oyster; but I'll take my oath on it, till he have made an oyster of me, he shall never make me such a fool. One woman is fair, yet I am well; another is wise, yet I am well; another virtuous, yet I am well: but till all graces be in one woman, one woman shall not come in my grace. Rich she shall be, that's certain; wise, or I'll none; virtuous, or I'll never cheapen her; fair, or I'll never look on her; mild, or come not near me; noble, or not I for an angel; of good discourse, an excellent musician, and her hair shall be of what colour it please God. Ha! the prince and Monsieur Love! I will hide me in the arbour.   [*Withdraws.*]

Enter DON PEDRO, CLAUDIO, *and* LEONATO.

D. PEDRO.   Come, shall we hear this music?
CLAUD.   Yea, my good lord. How still the evening is,
    As hush'd on purpose to grace harmony!
D. PEDRO.   See you where Benedick hath hid himself?
CLAUD.   O, very well, my lord: the music ended,
    We'll fit the kid-fox with a pennyworth.

Enter BALTHASAR *with Music.*

D. PEDRO.   Come, Balthasar, we'll hear that song again.
BALTH.   O, good my lord, tax not so bad a voice
    To slander music any more than once.
D. PEDRO.   It is the witness still of excellency
    To put a strange face on his own perfection.
    I pray thee, sing, and let me woo no more.
BALTH.   Because you talk of wooing, I will sing;
    Since many a wooer doth commence his suit
    To her he thinks not worthy, yet he wooes,
    Yet will he swear he loves.
D. PEDRO.   Nay, pray thee, come;
    Or, if thou wilt hold longer argument,
    Do it in notes.
BALTH.   Note this before my notes;
    There's not a note of mine that's worth the noting.
D. PEDRO.   Why, these are very crotchets[1] that he speaks;
    Note, notes, forsooth, and nothing.   [*Air.*]
BENE.   Now, divine air! now is his soul ravished! Is it not strange that
    sheeps' guts should hale souls out of men's bodies? Well, a horn for
    my money, when all's done.

BALTH.   The Song.

            Sigh no more, ladies, sigh no more,
              Men were deceivers ever,
            One foot in sea and one on shore,
              To one thing constant never:

---

1. *crotchets*] perverse conceits; also, characters in music.

> Then sigh not so, but let them go,
>   And be you blithe and bonny,
> Converting all your sounds of woe
>   Into Hey nonny, nonny.
>
> Sing no more ditties, sing no moe,
>   Of dumps so dull and heavy;
> The fraud of men was ever so,
>   Since summer first was leavy:[2]
>   Then sigh not so, &c.

D. PEDRO.   By my troth, a good song.

BALTH.   And an ill singer, my lord.

D. PEDRO.   Ha, no, no, faith; thou singest well enough for a shift.

BENE.   An[3] he had been a dog that should have howled thus, they would have hanged him: and I pray God his bad voice bode no mischief. I had as lief have heard the night-raven, come what plague could have come after it.

D. PEDRO.   Yea, marry, dost thou hear, Balthasar? I pray thee, get us some excellent music; for to-morrow night we would have it at the Lady Hero's chamber-window.

BALTH.   The best I can, my lord.

D. PEDRO.   Do so: farewell. [*Exit* BALTHASAR.] Come hither, Leonato. What was it you told me of to-day, that your niece Beatrice was in love with Signior Benedick?

CLAUD.   O, ay: stalk on, stalk on; the fowl sits. I did never think that lady would have loved any man.

LEON.   No, nor I neither; but most wonderful that she should so dote on Signior Benedick, whom she hath in all outward behaviours seemed ever to abhor.

BENE.   Is't possible? Sits the wind in that corner?

LEON.   By my troth, my lord, I cannot tell what to think of it, but that she loves him with an enraged affection; it is past the infinite of thought.

D. PEDRO.   May be she doth but counterfeit.

CLAUD.   Faith, like enough.

---

2. *leavy*] full of leaves.
3. *An*] if.

LEON.   O God, counterfeit! There was never counterfeit of passion came so near the life of passion as she discovers it.

D. PEDRO.   Why, what effects of passion shows she?

CLAUD.   Bait the hook well; this fish will bite.

LEON.   What effects, my lord? She will sit you, you heard my daughter tell you how.

CLAUD.   She did, indeed.

D. PEDRO.   How, how, I pray you? You amaze me: I would have thought her spirit had been invincible against all assaults of affection.

LEON.   I would have sworn it had, my lord; especially against Benedick.

BENE.   I should think this a gull,[4] but that the white-bearded fellow speaks it: knavery cannot, sure, hide himself in such reverence.

CLAUD.   He hath ta'en the infection: hold it up.

D. PEDRO.   Hath she made her affection known to Benedick?

LEON.   No; and swears she never will: that's her torment.

CLAUD.   'Tis true, indeed; so your daughter says: 'Shall I,' says she, 'that have so oft encountered him with scorn, write to him that I love him?'

LEON.   This says she now when she is beginning to write to him; for she'll be up twenty times a night; and there will she sit in her smock till she have writ a sheet of paper: my daughter tells us all.

CLAUD.   Now you talk of a sheet of paper, I remember a pretty jest your daughter told us of.

LEON.   O, when she had writ it, and was reading it over, she found Benedick and Beatrice between the sheet?

CLAUD.   That.

LEON.   O, she tore the letter into a thousand halfpence; railed at herself, that she should be so immodest to write to one that she knew would flout her; 'I measure him,' says she, 'by my own spirit; for I should flout him, if he writ to me; yea, though I love him, I should.'

CLAUD.   Then down upon her knees she falls, weeps, sobs, beats her heart, tears her hair, prays, curses; 'O sweet Benedick! God give me patience!'

---

4. *gull*] trick.

LEON.   She doth indeed; my daughter says so: and the ecstasy hath so much overborne her, that my daughter is sometime afeard she will do a desperate outrage to herself: it is very true.

D. PEDRO.   It were good that Benedick knew of it by some other, if she will not discover it.

CLAUD.   To what end? He would make but a sport of it, and torment the poor lady worse.

D. PEDRO.   An he should, it were an alms to hang him. She's an excellent sweet lady; and, out of all suspicion, she is virtuous.

CLAUD.   And she is exceeding wise.

D. PEDRO.   In every thing but in loving Benedick.

LEON.   O, my lord, wisdom and blood combating in so tender a body, we have ten proofs to one that blood hath the victory. I am sorry for her, as I have just cause, being her uncle and her guardian.

D. PEDRO.   I would she had bestowed this dotage on me: I would have daffed[5] all other respects, and made her half myself. I pray you, tell Benedick of it, and hear what a' will say.

LEON.   Were it good, think you?

CLAUD.   Hero thinks surely she will die; for she says she will die, if he love her not; and she will die, ere she make her love known; and she will die, if he woo her, rather than she will bate one breath of her accustomed crossness.

D. PEDRO.   She doth well: if she should make tender[6] of her love, 'tis very possible he'll scorn it; for the man, as you know all, hath a contemptible spirit.

CLAUD.   He is a very proper man.

D. PEDRO.   He hath indeed a good outward happiness.

CLAUD.   Before God! and in my mind, very wise.

D. PEDRO.   He doth indeed show some sparks that are like wit.

CLAUD.   And I take him to be valiant.

D. PEDRO.   As Hector, I assure you: and in the managing of quarrels you may say he is wise; for either he avoids them with great discretion, or undertakes them with a most Christian-like fear.

LEON.   If he do fear God, a' must necessarily keep peace: if he break the peace, he ought to enter into a quarrel with fear and trembling.

---

5. *daffed*] doffed, put aside.
6. *tender*] an offer for acceptance.

D. PEDRO.   And so will he do; for the man doth fear God, howsoever it
    seems not in him by some large jests he will make. Well, I am sorry
    for your niece. Shall we go seek Benedick, and tell him of her love?
CLAUD.   Never tell him, my lord: let her wear it out with good counsel.
LEON.   Nay, that's impossible: she may wear her heart out first.
D. PEDRO.   Well, we will hear further of it by your daughter: let it cool
    the while. I love Benedick well; and I could wish he would modestly
    examine himself, to see how much he is unworthy so good a lady.
LEON.   My lord, will you walk? dinner is ready.
CLAUD.   If he do not dote on her upon this, I will never trust my
    expectation.
D. PEDRO.   Let there be the same net spread for her; and that must
    your daughter and her gentlewomen carry. The sport will be, when
    they hold one an opinion of another's dotage, and no such matter:
    that's the scene that I would see, which will be merely a dumb-
    show. Let us send her to call him in to dinner.

              [*Exeunt* DON PEDRO, CLAUDIO, *and* LEONATO.]
BENE.   [*Coming forward*] This can be no trick: the conference was sadly
    borne. They have the truth of this from Hero. They seem to pity the
    lady: it seems her affections have their full bent. Love me! why, it
    must be requited. I hear how I am censured: they say I will bear
    myself proudly, if I perceive the love come from her; they say too that
    she will rather die than give any sign of affection. I did never think to
    marry: I must not seem proud: happy are they that hear their detrac-
    tions, and can put them to mending. They say the lady is fair, — 'tis a
    truth, I can bear them witness; and virtuous, — 'tis so, I cannot re-
    prove it; and wise, but for loving me, — by my troth, it is no addition to
    her wit, nor no great argument of her folly, for I will be horribly in
    love with her. I may chance have some odd quirks and remnants of
    wit broken on me, because I have railed so long against marriage: but
    doth not the appetite alter? a man loves the meat in his youth that he
    cannot endure in his age. Shall quips and sentences and these paper
    bullets[7] of the brain awe a man from the career of his humour? No,
    the world must be peopled. When I said I would die a bachelor, I did
    not think I should live till I were married. Here comes Beatrice. By
    this day! she's a fair lady: I do spy some marks of love in her.

---

7. *paper bullets*] epigrams from books.

Enter BEATRICE.

BEAT.   Against my will I am sent to bid you come in to dinner.

BENE.   Fair Beatrice, I thank you for your pains.

BEAT.   I took no more pains for those thanks than you take pains to
thank me: if it had been painful, I would not have come.

BENE.   You take pleasure, then, in the message?

BEAT.   Yea, just so much as you may take upon a knife's point, and
choke a daw withal. You have no stomach, signior: fare you well.

[*Exit.*]

BENE.   Ha! 'Against my will I am sent to bid you come in to dinner;'
there's a double meaning in that. 'I took no more pains for those
thanks than you took pains to thank me;' that's as much as to say,
Any pains that I take for you is as easy as thanks. If I do not take pity
of her, I am a villain; if I do not love her, I am a Jew. I will go get her
picture.

[*Exit.*]

ACT III.

SCENE I. LEONATO'S *orchard*.

Enter HERO, MARGARET, *and* URSULA.

HERO. Good Margaret, run thee to the parlour;
    There shalt thou find my cousin Beatrice
    Proposing with the prince and Claudio:
    Whisper her ear, and tell her, I and Ursula
    Walk in the orchard, and our whole discourse
    Is all of her; say that thou overheard'st us;
    And bid her steal into the pleached bower,
    Where honeysuckles, ripen'd by the sun,
    Forbid the sun to enter; like favourites,
    Made proud by princes, that advance their pride
    Against that power that bred it: there will she hide her,
    To listen our propose. This is thy office;
    Bear thee well in it, and leave us alone.
MARG. I'll make her come, I warrant you, presently.   [*Exit.*]
HERO. Now, Ursula, when Beatrice doth come,
    As we do trace this alley up and down,
    Our talk must only be of Benedick.
    When I do name him, let it be thy part
    To praise him more than ever man did merit:
    My talk to thee must be, how Benedick
    Is sick in love with Beatrice. Of this matter
    Is little Cupid's crafty arrow made,
    That only wounds by hearsay.

Enter BEATRICE, *behind.*

                          Now begin;
    For look where Beatrice, like a lapwing, runs
    Close by the ground, to hear our conference.
URS.   The pleasant'st angling is to see the fish
    Cut with her golden oars the silver stream,
    And greedily devour the treacherous bait:
    So angle we for Beatrice; who even now
    Is couched in the woodbine coverture.
    Fear you not my part of the dialogue.
HERO.   Then go we near her, that her ear lose nothing
    Of the false sweet bait that we lay for it.

                              [*Approaching the bower.*]

    No, truly, Ursula, she is too disdainful;
    I know her spirits are as coy and wild
    As haggerds[1] of the rock.
URS.   But are you sure
    That Benedick loves Beatrice so entirely?
HERO.   So says the prince and my new-trothed lord.
URS.   And did they bid you tell her of it, madam?
HERO.   They did entreat me to acquaint her of it;
    But I persuaded them, if they loved Benedick,
    To wish him wrestle with affection,
    And never to let Beatrice know of it.
URS.   Why did you so? Doth not the gentleman
    Deserve as full as fortunate a bed
    As ever Beatrice shall couch upon?
HERO.   O god of love! I know he doth deserve
    As much as may be yielded to a man:
    But Nature never framed a woman's heart
    Of prouder stuff than that of Beatrice;
    Disdain and scorn ride sparkling in her eyes,
    Misprising what they look on; and her wit
    Values itself so highly, that to her
    All matter else seems weak: she cannot love,

---

1. *haggerds*] haggards; wild, untrained hawks.

Nor take no shape nor project of affection,
She is so self-endeared.

URS.   Sure, I think so;
And therefore certainly it were not good
She knew his love, lest she make sport at it.

HERO.   Why, you speak truth. I never yet saw man,
How wise, how noble, young, how rarely featured,
But she would spell him backward: if fair-faced,
She would swear the gentleman should be her sister;
If black, why, Nature, drawing of an antique,
Made a foul blot; if tall, a lance ill-headed;
If low, an agate very vilely cut;
If speaking, why, a vane blown with all winds;
If silent, why, a block moved with none.
So turns she every man the wrong side out;
And never gives to truth and virtue that
Which simpleness and merit purchaseth.

URS.   Sure, sure, such carping is not commendable.

HERO.   No, not to be so odd, and from all fashions,
As Beatrice is, cannot be commendable:
But who dare tell her so? If I should speak,
She would mock me into air; O, she would laugh me
Out of myself, press me to death with wit!
Therefore let Benedick, like cover'd fire,
Consume away in sighs, waste inwardly:
It were a better death than die with mocks,
Which is as bad as die with tickling.

URS.   Yet tell her of it: hear what she will say.

HERO.   No; rather I will go to Benedick,
And counsel him to fight against his passion.
And, truly, I'll devise some honest slanders
To stain my cousin with: one doth not know
How much an ill word may empoison liking.

URS.   O, do not do your cousin such a wrong!
She cannot be so much without true judgement,—
Having so swift and excellent a wit
As she is prized to have,—as to refuse
So rare a gentleman as Signior Benedick.

HERO.   He is the only man of Italy,

Always excepted my dear Claudio.

URS. I pray you, be not angry with me, madam,
  Speaking my fancy: Signior Benedick,
  For shape, for bearing, argument and valour,
  Goes foremost in report through Italy.

HERO. Indeed, he hath an excellent good name.

URS. His excellence did earn it, ere he had it.
  When are you married, madam?

HERO. Why, every day, to-morrow. Come, go in:
  I'll show thee some attires; and have thy counsel
  Which is the best to furnish me to-morrow.

URS. She's limed,[2] I warrant you: we have caught her, madam.

HERO. If it prove so, then loving goes by haps:
  Some Cupid kills with arrows, some with traps.

           [*Exeunt* HERO *and* URSULA.]

BEAT. [*Coming forward*] What fire is in mine ears? Can this be true?
  Stand I condemn'd for pride and scorn so much?
  Contempt, farewell! and maiden pride, adieu!
   No glory lives behind the back of such.
  And, Benedick, love on; I will requite thee,
   Taming my wild heart to thy loving hand:
  If thou dost love, my kindness shall incite thee
   To bind our loves up in a holy band;
  For others say thou dost deserve, and I
  Believe it better than reportingly.   [*Exit.*]

SCENE II. *A room in* LEONATO'S *house.*

Enter DON PEDRO, CLAUDIO, BENEDICK, *and* LEONATO.

D. PEDRO. I do but stay till your marriage be consummate, and then
  go I toward Arragon.

CLAUD. I'll bring you thither, my lord, if you'll vouchsafe me.

---

2. *limed*] trapped, ensnared as a bird with birdlime, a glutinous substance used to catch
 birds.

D. PEDRO.   Nay, that would be as great a soil in the new gloss of your marriage, as to show a child his new coat and forbid him to wear it. I will only be bold with Benedick for his company; for, from the crown of his head to the sole of his foot, he is all mirth: he hath twice or thrice cut Cupid's bow-string, and the little hangman dare not shoot at him; he hath a heart as sound as a bell, and his tongue is the clapper, for what his heart thinks his tongue speaks.

BENE.   Gallants, I am not as I have been.

LEON.   So say I: methinks you are sadder.

CLAUD.   I hope he be in love.

D. PEDRO.   Hang him, truant! there's no true drop of blood in him, to be truly touched with love; if he be sad, he wants money.

BENE.   I have the toothache.

D. PEDRO.   Draw it.

BENE.   Hang it!

CLAUD.   You must hang it first, and draw it afterwards.[1]

D. PEDRO.   What! sigh for the toothache?

LEON.   Where is but a humour or a worm.

BENE.   Well, every one can master a grief but he that has it.

CLAUD.   Yet say I, he is in love.

D. PEDRO.   There is no appearance of fancy in him, unless it be a fancy that he hath to strange disguises; as, to be a Dutchman to-day, a Frenchman to-morrow; or in the shape of two countries at once, as, a German from the waist downward, all slops,[2] and a Spaniard from the hip upward, no doublet. Unless he have a fancy to this foolery, as it appears he hath, he is no fool for fancy, as you would have it appear he is.

CLAUD.   If he be not in love with some woman, there is no believing old signs: a' brushes his hat o' mornings; what should that bode?

D. PEDRO.   Hath any man seen him at the barber's?

CLAUD.   No, but the barber's man hath been seen with him; and the old ornament of his cheek hath already stuffed tennis-balls.

LEON.   Indeed, he looks younger than he did, by the loss of a beard.

---

1. *You must hang ... afterwards*] an allusion to the punishment of "drawing," i.e., disembowelment, which followed hanging and preceded "quartering" (dividing the body into four parts) in convictions of treason.

2. *slops*] loose, ill-fitting trousers.

D. PEDRO. Nay, a' rubs himself with civet:[3] can you smell him out by that?

CLAUD. That's as much as to say, the sweet youth's in love.

D. PEDRO. The greatest note of it is his melancholy.

CLAUD. And when was he wont to wash his face?

D. PEDRO. Yea, or to paint himself? for the which, I hear what they say of him.

CLAUD. Nay, but his jesting spirit; which is now crept into a lute-string, and now governed by stops.[4]

D. PEDRO. Indeed, that tells a heavy tale for him: conclude, conclude he is in love.

CLAUD. Nay, but I know who loves him.

D. PEDRO. That would I know too: I warrant, one that knows him not.

CLAUD. Yes, and his ill conditions; and, in despite of all, dies for him.

D. PEDRO. She shall be buried with her face upwards.

BENE. Yet is this no charm for the toothache. Old signior, walk aside with me: I have studied eight or nine wise words to speak to you, which these hobby-horses must not hear.

[*Exeunt* BENEDICK *and* LEONATO.]

D. PEDRO. For my life, to break with him about Beatrice.

CLAUD. 'Tis even so. Hero and Margaret have by this played their parts with Beatrice; and then the two bears will not bite one another when they meet.

Enter DON JOHN.

D. JOHN. My lord and brother, God save you!

D. PEDRO. Good den,[5] brother.

D. JOHN. If your leisure served, I would speak with you.

D. PEDRO. In private?

D. JOHN. If it please you: yet Count Claudio may hear; for what I would speak of concerns him.

D. PEDRO. What's the matter?

D. JOHN. [*To* CLAUDIO] Means your lordship to be married to-morrow?

---

3. *civet*] a perfume from the civet-cat.
4. *stops*] marks on the lute's fingerboard that indicate where the fingers should be pressed to produce various notes.
5. *den*] abbreviation for evening.

D. PEDRO.   You know he does.

D. JOHN.   I know not that, when he knows what I know.

CLAUD.   If there be any impediment, I pray you discover it.

D. JOHN.   You may think I love you not: let that appear hereafter, and aim better at me by that I now will manifest. For my brother, I think he holds you well, and in dearness of heart hath holp to effect your ensuing marriage,—surely suit ill spent and labour ill bestowed.

D. PEDRO.   Why, what's the matter?

D. JOHN.   I came hither to tell you; and, circumstances shortened, for she has been too long a talking of, the lady is disloyal.

CLAUD.   Who, Hero?

D. JOHN.   Even she; Leonato's Hero, your Hero, every man's Hero.

CLAUD.   Disloyal?

D. JOHN.   The word is too good to paint out her wickedness; I could say she were worse: think you of a worse title, and I will fit her to it. Wonder not till further warrant: go but with me to-night, you shall see her chamber-window entered, even the night before her wedding-day: if you love her then, to-morrow wed her; but it would better fit your honour to change your mind.

CLAUD.   May this be so?

D. PEDRO.   I will not think it.

D. JOHN.   If you dare not trust that you see, confess not that you know: if you will follow me, I will show you enough; and when you have seen more, and heard more, proceed accordingly.

CLAUD.   If I see any thing to-night why I should not marry her to-morrow, in the congregation, where I should wed, there will I shame her.

D. PEDRO.   And, as I wooed for thee to obtain her, I will join with thee to disgrace her.

D. JOHN.   I will disparage her no farther till you are my witnesses: bear it coldly but till midnight, and let the issue show itself.

D. PEDRO.   O day untowardly turned!

CLAUD.   O mischief strangely thwarting!

D. JOHN.   O plague right well prevented! so will you say when you have seen the sequel.   [*Exeunt.*]

SCENE III. *A street*.

Enter DOGBERRY *and* VERGES *with the* Watch.

DOG. Are you good men and true?

VERG. Yea, or else it were pity but they should suffer salvation, body and soul.

DOG. Nay, that were a punishment too good for them, if they should have any allegiance in them, being chosen for the prince's watch.

VERG. Well, give them their charge, neighbour Dogberry.

DOG. First, who think you the most desartless man to be constable?

FIRST WATCH. Hugh Otecake, sir, or George Seacole; for they can write and read.

DOG. Come hither, neighbour Seacole. God hath blessed you with a good name: to be a well-favoured man is the gift of fortune; but to write and read comes by nature.

SEC. WATCH. Both which, master constable,—

DOG. You have: I knew it would be your answer. Well, for your favour, sir, why, give God thanks, and make no boast of it; and for your writing and reading, let that appear when there is no need of such vanity. You are thought here to be the most senseless[1] and fit man for the constable of the watch; therefore bear you the lantern. This is your charge: you shall comprehend[2] all vagrom[3] men; you are to bid any man stand, in the prince's name.

SEC. WATCH. How if a' will not stand?

DOG. Why, then, take no note of him, but let him go; and presently call the rest of the watch together, and thank God you are rid of a knave.

VERG. If he will not stand when he is bidden, he is none of the prince's subjects.

---

1. *senseless*] i.e., sensible.
2. *comprehend*] i.e., apprehend.
3. *vagrom*] i.e., vagrant.

DOG. True, and they are to meddle with none but the prince's sub-
       jects. You shall also make no noise in the streets; for for the watch to
       babble and to talk is most tolerable[4] and not to be endured.
WATCH. We will rather sleep than talk: we know what belongs to a
       watch.
DOG. Why, you speak like an ancient and most quiet watchman; for I
       cannot see how sleeping should offend: only, have a care that your
       bills[5] be not stolen. Well, you are to call at all the ale-houses, and
       bid those that are drunk get them to bed.
WATCH. How if they will not?
DOG. Why, then, let them alone till they are sober: if they make you
       not then the better answer, you may say they are not the men you
       took them for.
WATCH. Well, sir.
DOG. If you meet a thief, you may suspect him, by virtue of your
       office, to be no true man; and, for such kind of men, the less you
       meddle or make with them, why, the more is for your honesty.
WATCH. If we know him to be a thief, shall we not lay hands on him?
DOG. Truly, by your office, you may; but I think they that touch pitch
       will be defiled: the most peaceable way for you, if you do take a thief,
       is to let him show himself what he is, and steal out of your company.
VERG. You have been always called a merciful man, partner.
DOG. Truly, I would not hang a dog by my will, much more a man
       who hath any honesty in him.
VERG. If you hear a child cry in the night, you must call to the nurse
       and bid her still it.
WATCH. How if the nurse be asleep and will not hear us?
DOG. Why, then, depart in peace, and let the child wake her with
       crying; for the ewe that will not hear her lamb when it baes will
       never answer a calf when he bleats.
VERG. 'Tis very true.
DOG. This is the end of the charge:—you, constable, are to present
       the prince's own person: if you meet the prince in the night, you
       may stay him.

---

4. *tolerable*] i.e., intolerable.
5. *bills*] a kind of pike or halbert.

VERG. Nay, by'r lady, that I think a' cannot.

DOG. Five shillings to one on't, with any man that knows the statues, he may stay him: marry, not without the prince be willing; for, indeed, the watch ought to offend no man; and it is an offence to stay a man against his will.

VERG. By'r lady, I think it be so.

DOG. Ha, ah, ha! Well, masters, good night: an there be any matter of weight chances, call up me: keep your fellows' counsels and your own; and good night. Come, neighbour.

WATCH. Well, masters, we hear our charge: let us go sit here upon the church-bench till two, and then all to bed.

DOG. One word more, honest neighbours. I pray you, watch about Signior Leonato's door; for the wedding being there to-morrow, there is a great coil to-night. Adieu: be vigitant,[6] I beseech you.

[*Exeunt* DOGBERRY *and* VERGES.]

Enter BORACHIO *and* CONRADE.

BORA. What, Conrade!

WATCH. [*Aside*] Peace! stir not.

BORA. Conrade, I say!

CON. Here, man; I am at thy elbow.

BORA. Mass, and my elbow itched; I thought there would a scab follow.

CON. I will owe thee an answer for that: and now forward with thy tale.

BORA. Stand thee close, then, under this pent-house, for it drizzles rain; and I will, like a true drunkard, utter all to thee.

WATCH. [*Aside*] Some treason, masters: yet stand close.

BORA. Therefore know I have earned of Don John a thousand ducats.

CON. Is it possible that any villany should be so dear?

BORA. Thou shouldst rather ask, if it were possible any villany should be so rich; for when rich villains have need of poor ones, poor ones may make what price they will.

CON. I wonder at it.

BORA. That shows thou art unconfirmed. Thou knowest that the fashion of a doublet, or a hat, or a cloak, is nothing to a man.

---

6. *vigitant*] i.e., vigilant.

CON.   Yes, it is apparel.

BORA.   I mean, the fashion.

CON.   Yes, the fashion is the fashion.

BORA.   Tush! I may as well say the fool's the fool. But seest thou not
what a deformed thief this fashion is?

WATCH.   [*Aside*] I know that Deformed; a' has been a vile thief this
seven year; a' goes up and down like a gentleman: I remember his
name.

BORA.   Didst thou not hear somebody?

CON.   No; 'twas the vane on the house.

BORA.   Seest thou not, I say, what a deformed thief this fashion is?
how giddily a' turns about all the hot bloods between fourteen
and five-and-thirty? sometimes fashioning them like Pharaoh's
soldiers in the reechy[7] painting, sometime like god Bel's priests in
the old church-window, sometime like the shaven Hercules in the
smirched worm-eaten tapestry, where his codpiece seems as
massy as his club?

CON.   All this I see; and I see that the fashion wears out more apparel
than the man. But art not thou thyself giddy with the fashion too,
that thou hast shifted out of thy tale into telling me of the fashion?

BORA.   Not so, neither: but know that I have to-night wooed Margaret,
the Lady Hero's gentlewoman, by the name of Hero: she leans me
out at her mistress' chamber-window, bids me a thousand times good
night,—I tell this tale vilely:—I should first tell thee how the prince,
Claudio and my master, planted and placed and possessed by my
master Don John, saw afar off in the orchard this amiable encounter.

CON.   And thought they Margaret was Hero?

BORA.   Two of them did, the prince and Claudio; but the devil my
master knew she was Margaret; and partly by his oaths, which first
possessed them, partly by the dark night, which did deceive them,
but chiefly by my villany, which did confirm any slander that Don
John had made, away went Claudio enraged; swore he would meet
her, as he was appointed, next morning at the temple, and there,
before the whole congregation, shame her with what he saw o'er
night, and send her home again without a husband.

---

7. *reechy*] dirty, filthy.

FIRST WATCH.   We charge you, in the prince's name, stand!

SEC. WATCH.   Call up the right master constable. We have here recovered the most dangerous piece of lechery that ever was known in the commonwealth.

FIRST WATCH.   And one Deformed is one of them: I know him; a' wears a lock.[8]

CON.   Masters, masters,—

SEC. WATCH.   You'll be made bring Deformed forth, I warrant you.

CON.   Masters,—

FIRST WATCH.   Never speak: we charge you let us obey you to go with us.

BORA.   We are like to prove a goodly commodity, being taken up of these men's bills.

CON.   A commodity in question, I warrant you. Come, we'll obey you.

[*Exeunt.*]

SCENE IV. HERO'S *apartment.*

Enter HERO, MARGARET, *and* URSULA.

HERO.   Good Ursula, wake my cousin Beatrice, and desire her to rise.

URS.   I will, lady.

HERO.   And bid her come hither.

URS.   Well.   [*Exit.*]

MARG.   Troth, I think your other rabato[1] were better.

HERO.   No, pray thee, good Meg, I'll wear this.

MARG.   By my troth's not so good; and I warrant your cousin will say so.

HERO.   My cousin's a fool, and thou art another: I'll wear none but this.

---

8. *lock*] a "love-lock": a ringlet of hair tied with a ribbon worn near the left ear by young men about town.

1. *rabato*] the word is used both for a ruff (stiff collar) and for the wire-support of the ruff.

MARG.   I like the new tire[2] within excellently, if the hair were a
thought browner; and your gown's a most rare fashion, i' faith. I saw
the Duchess of Milan's gown that they praise so.

HERO.   O, that exceeds, they say.

MARG.   By my troth's but a night-gown in respect of yours,—cloth o'
gold, and cuts, and laced with silver, set with pearls, down sleeves,
side sleeves, and skirts, round underborne with a bluish tinsel: but
for a fine, quaint, graceful and excellent fashion, yours is worth ten
on't.

HERO.   God give me joy to wear it! for my heart is exceeding heavy.

MARG.   'Twill be heavier soon by the weight of a man.

HERO.   Fie upon thee! art not ashamed?

MARG.   Of what, lady? of speaking honourably? Is not marriage honourable in a beggar? Is not your lord honourable without marriage?
I think you would have me say, 'saving your reverence, a husband:'
an bad thinking do not wrest true speaking, I'll offend nobody: is
there any harm in 'the heavier for a husband'? None, I think, an it
be the right husband and the right wife; otherwise 'tis light, and not
heavy: ask my Lady Beatrice else; here she comes.

Enter BEATRICE.

HERO.   Good morrow, coz.

BEAT.   Good morrow, sweet Hero.

HERO.   Why, how now? do you speak in the sick tune?

BEAT.   I am out of all other tune, methinks.

MARG.   Clap's into 'Light o' love;' that goes without a burden: do you
sing it, and I'll dance it.

BEAT.   Ye light o' love, with your heels! then, if your husband have
stables enough, you'll see he shall lack no barns.

MARG.   O illegitimate construction! I scorn that with my heels.

BEAT.   'Tis almost five o'clock, cousin; 'tis time you were ready. By my
troth, I am exceeding ill: heigh-ho!

MARG.   For a hawk, a horse, or a husband?

BEAT.   For the letter that begins them all, H.

---

2. *tire*] headdress or cap to which false hair was attached.

MARG.   Well, an you be not turned Turk, there's no more sailing by the star.

BEAT.   What means the fool, trow?

MARG.   Nothing I; but God send every one their heart's desire!

HERO.   These gloves the count sent me; they are an excellent perfume.

BEAT.   I am stuffed, cousin; I cannot smell.

MARG.   A maid, and stuffed! there's goodly catching of cold.

BEAT.   O, God help me! God help me! how long have you professed apprehension?

MARG.   Ever since you left it. Doth not my wit become me rarely?

BEAT.   It is not seen enough, you should wear it in your cap. By my troth, I am sick.

MARG.   Get you some of this distilled Carduus Benedictus, and lay it to your heart: it is the only thing for a qualm.

HERO.   There thou prickest her with a thistle.

BEAT.   Benedictus! why Benedictus? you have some moral in this Benedictus.

MARG.   Moral! no, by my troth, I have no moral meaning; I meant, plain holy-thistle. You may think perchance that I think you are in love: nay, by'r lady, I am not such a fool to think what I list; nor I list not to think what I can; nor, indeed, I cannot think, if I would think my heart out of thinking, that you are in love, or that you will be in love, or that you can be in love. Yet Benedick was such another, and now is he become a man: he swore he would never marry; and yet now, in despite of his heart, he eats his meat without grudging: and how you may be converted, I know not; but methinks you look with your eyes as other women do.

BEAT.   What pace is this that thy tongue keeps?

MARG.   Not a false gallop.

Re-enter URSULA.

URS.   Madam, withdraw: the prince, the count, Signior Benedick, Don John, and all the gallants of the town, are come to fetch you to church.

HERO.   Help to dress me, good coz, good Meg, good Ursula. [*Exeunt.*]

SCENE V. *Another room in* LEONATO'S *house.*

Enter LEONATO, *with* DOGBERRY *and* VERGES.

LEON. What would you with me, honest neighbour?

DOG. Marry, sir, I would have some confidence[1] with you that decerns[2] you nearly.

LEON. Brief, I pray you; for you see it is a busy time with me.

DOG. Marry, this it is, sir.

VERG. Yes, in truth it is, sir.

LEON. What is it, my good friends?

DOG. Goodman Verges, sir, speaks a little off the matter: an old man,
sir, and his wits are not so blunt as, God help, I would desire they
were; but, in faith, honest as the skin between his brows.

VERG. Yes, I thank God I am as honest as any man living that is an old
man and no honester than I.

DOG. Comparisons are odorous:[3] palabras,[4] neighbour Verges.

LEON. Neighbours, you are tedious.

DOG. It pleases your worship to say so, but we are the poor duke's
officers; but truly, for mine own part, if I were as tedious as a king, I
could find in my heart to bestow it all of your worship.

LEON. All thy tediousness on me, ah?

DOG. Yea, an 'twere a thousand pound more than 'tis; for I hear as
good exclamation[5] on your worship as of any man in the city; and
though I be but a poor man, I am glad to hear it.

VERG. And so am I.

LEON. I would fain know what you have to say.

---

1. *confidence*] probably for "conference."
2. *decerns*] i.e., concerns.
3. *odorous*] i.e., odious.
4. *palabras*] *pocas palabras*, few words.
5. *exclamation*] possibly for "acclamation."

VERG. Marry, sir, our watch to-night, excepting your worship's presence, ha' ta'en a couple of as arrant knaves as any in Messina.

DOG. A good old man, sir; he will be talking: as they say, When the age is in, the wit is out: God help us! it is a world to see. Well said, i' faith, neighbour Verges: well, God's a good man; an two men ride of a horse, one must ride behind. An honest soul, i' faith, sir; by my troth he is, as ever broke bread; but God is to be worshipped; all men are not alike; alas, good neighbour!

LEON. Indeed, neighbour, he comes too short of you.

DOG. Gifts that God gives.

LEON. I must leave you.

DOG. One word, sir: our watch, sir, have indeed comprehended two aspicious[6] persons, and we would have them this morning examined before your worship.

LEON. Take their examination yourself, and bring it me: I am now in great haste, as it may appear unto you.

DOG. It shall be suffigance.[7]

LEON. Drink some wine ere you go: fare you well.

Enter a Messenger.

MESS. My lord, they stay for you to give your daughter to her husband.

LEON. I'll wait upon them: I am ready.

[*Exeunt* LEONATO *and* MESSENGER.]

DOG. Go, good partner, go, get you to Francis[8] Seacole; bid him bring his pen and inkhorn to the gaol: we are now to examination these men.

VERG. And we must do it wisely.

DOG. We will spare for no wit, I warrant you; here's that shall drive some of them to a noncome: only get the learned writer to set down our excommunication, and meet me at the gaol. [*Exeunt.*]

---

6. *aspicious*] i.e., suspicious.
7. *suffigance*] i.e., sufficient.
8. *Francis*] earlier, Seacole's first name is given as George (Act III, scene iii).

ACT IV.

SCENE I. A *church*.

Enter DON PEDRO, DON JOHN, LEONATO, FRIAR FRANCIS, CLAUDIO, BENEDICK, HERO, BEATRICE, *and* Attendants.

LEON. Come, Friar Francis, be brief; only to the plain form of marriage, and you shall recount their particular duties afterwards.

FRIAR. You come hither, my lord, to marry this lady.

CLAUD. No.

LEON. To be married to her: friar, you come to marry her.

FRIAR. Lady, you come hither to be married to this count.

HERO. I do.

FRIAR. If either of you know any inward impediment why you should not be conjoined, I charge you, on your souls, to utter it.

CLAUD. Know you any, Hero?

HERO. None, my lord.

FRIAR. Know you any, count?

LEON. I dare make his answer, none.

CLAUD. O, what men dare do! what men may do! what men daily do, not knowing what they do!

BENE. How now! interjections? Why, then, some be of laughing, as, ah, ha, he!

CLAUD. Stand thee by, friar. Father, by your leave:
Will you with free and unconstrained soul
Give me this maid, your daughter?

LEON. As freely, son, as God did give her me.

CLAUD. And what have I to give you back, whose worth
May counterpoise this rich and precious gift?

47

D. PEDRO.   Nothing, unless you render her again.

CLAUD.   Sweet prince, you learn me noble thankfulness.
There, Leonato, take her back again:
Give not this rotten orange to your friend;
She's but the sign and semblance of her honour.
Behold how like a maid she blushes here!
O, what authority and show of truth
Can cunning sin cover itself withal!
Comes not that blood as modest evidence
To witness simple virtue? Would you not swear,
All you that see her, that she were a maid,
By these exterior shows? But she is none:
She knows the heat of a luxurious bed;
Her blush is guiltiness, not modesty.

LEON.   What do you mean, my lord?

CLAUD.   Not to be married,
Not to knit my soul to an approved wanton.

LEON.   Dear my lord, if you, in your own proof,
Have vanquish'd the resistance of her youth,
And made defeat of her virginity,—

CLAUD.   I know what you would say: if I have known her,
You will say she did embrace me as a husband,
And so extenuate the 'forehand sin:
No, Leonato,
I never tempted her with word too large;
But, as a brother to his sister, show'd
Bashful sincerity and comely love.

HERO.   And seem'd I ever otherwise to you?

CLAUD.   Out on thee! Seeming! I will write against it:
You seem to me as Dian in her orb,
As chaste as is the bud ere it be blown;
But you are more intemperate in your blood
Than Venus, or those pamper'd animals
That rage in savage sensuality.

HERO.   Is my lord well, that he doth speak so wide?

LEON.   Sweet prince, why speak not you?

D. PEDRO.   What should I speak?
I stand dishonour'd, that have gone about

To link my dear friend to a common stale.[1]
LEON.   Are these things spoken, or do I but dream?
D. JOHN.   Sir, they are spoken, and these things are true.
BENE.   This looks not like a nuptial.
HERO.   True! O God!
CLAUD.   Leonato, stand I here?
    Is this the prince? is this the prince's brother?
    Is this face Hero's? are our eyes our own?
LEON.   All this is so: but what of this, my lord?
CLAUD.   Let me but move one question to your daughter;
    And, by that fatherly and kindly power
    That you have in her, bid her answer truly.
LEON.   I charge thee do so, as thou art my child.
HERO.   O, God defend me! how am I beset!
    What kind of catechising call you this?
CLAUD.   To make you answer truly to your name.
HERO.   Is it not Hero? Who can blot that name
    With any just reproach?
CLAUD.   Marry, that can Hero;
    Hero itself can blot out Hero's virtue.
    What man was he talk'd with you yesternight
    Out at your window betwixt twelve and one?
    Now, if you are a maid, answer to this.
HERO.   I talk'd with no man at that hour, my lord.
D. PEDRO.   Why, then are you no maiden. Leonato,
    I am sorry you must hear: upon mine honour,
    Myself, my brother, and this grieved count
    Did see her, hear her, at that hour last night
    Talk with a ruffian at her chamber-window;
    Who hath indeed, most like a liberal villain,
    Confess'd the vile encounters they have had
    A thousand times in secret.
D. JOHN.   Fie, fie! they are not to be named, my lord,
   · Not to be spoke of;

---

1. *stale*] something worn out by use; i.e., a prostitute.

There is not chastity enough in language,
Without offence to utter them. Thus, pretty lady,
I am sorry for thy much misgovernment.

CLAUD.   O Hero, what a Hero hadst thou been,
If half thy outward graces had been placed
About thy thoughts and counsels of thy heart!
But fare thee well, most foul, most fair! farewell,
Thou pure impiety and impious purity!
For thee I'll lock up all the gates of love,
And on my eyelids shall conjecture hang,
To turn all beauty into thoughts of harm,
And never shall it more be gracious.

LEON.   Hath no man's dagger here a point for me?   [HERO *swoons*.]

BEAT.   Why, how now, cousin! wherefore sink you down?

D. JOHN.   Come, let us go. These things, come thus to light,
Smother her spirits up.

[*Exeunt* DON PEDRO, DON JOHN, *and* CLAUDIO.]

BENE.   How doth the lady?

BEAT.   Dead, I think. Help, uncle!
Hero! why, Hero! Uncle! Signior Benedick! Friar!

LEON.   O Fate! take not away thy heavy hand.
Death is the fairest cover for her shame
That may be wish'd for.

BEAT.   How now, cousin Hero!

FRIAR.   Have comfort, lady.

LEON.   Dost thou look up?

FRIAR.   Yea, wherefore should she not?

LEON.   Wherefore! Why, doth not every earthly thing
Cry shame upon her? Could she here deny
The story that is printed in her blood?
Do not live, Hero; do not ope thine eyes:
For, did I think thou wouldst not quickly die,
Thought I thy spirits were stronger than thy shames,
Myself would, on the rearward of reproaches,
Strike at thy life. Grieved I, I had but one?
Chid I for that at frugal nature's frame?
O, one too much by thee! Why had I one?
Why ever wast thou lovely in my eyes?

Why had I not with charitable hand
Took up a beggar's issue at my gates,
Who smirched thus and mired with infamy,
I might·have said, 'No part of it is mine;
This shame derives itself from unknown loins'?
But mine, and mine I loved, and mine I praised,
And mine that I was proud on, mine so much
That I myself was to myself not mine,
Valuing of her,—why, she, O, she is fallen
Into a pit of ink, that the wide sea
Hath drops too few to wash her clean again,
And salt too little which may season give
To her foul-tainted flesh!

BENE.   Sir, sir, be patient.
For my part, I am so attired in wonder,
I know not what to say.

BEAT.   O, on my soul, my cousin is belied!

BENE.   Lady, were you her bedfellow last night?

BEAT.   No, truly, not; although, until last night,
I have this twelvemonth been her bedfellow.

LEON.   Confirm'd, confirm'd! O, that is stronger made
Which was before barr'd up with ribs of iron!
Would the two princes lie, and Claudio lie,
Who loved her so, that, speaking of her foulness,
Wash'd it with tears? Hence from her! let her die.

FRIAR.   Hear me a little;
For I have only been silent so long,
And given way unto this course of fortune,
By noting of the lady: I have mark'd
A thousand blushing apparitions
To start into her face; a thousand innocent shames
In angel whiteness beat away those blushes;
And in her eye there hath appear'd a fire,
To burn the errors that these princes hold
Against her maiden truth. Call me a fool;
Trust not my reading nor my observations,
Which with experimental seal doth warrant
The tenour of my book; trust not my age,

My reverence, calling, nor divinity,
If this sweet lady lie not guiltless here
Under some biting error.

LEON.   Friar, it cannot be.
Thou seest that all the grace that she hath left
Is that she will not add to her damnation
A sin of perjury; she not denies it:
Why seek'st thou, then, to cover with excuse
That which appears in proper nakedness?

FRIAR.   Lady, what man is he you are accused of?

HERO.   They know that do accuse me; I know none:
If I know more of any man alive
Than that which maiden modesty doth warrant,
Let all my sins lack mercy! O my father,
Prove you that any man with me conversed
At hours unmeet, or that I yesternight
Maintain'd the change of words with any creature,
Refuse me, hate me, torture me to death!

FRIAR.   There is some strange misprision in the princes.

BENE.   Two of them have the very bent of honour;
And if their wisdoms be misled in this,
The practice of it lives in John the bastard,
Whose spirits toil in frame of villanies.

LEON.   I know not. If they speak but truth of her,
These hands shall tear her; if they wrong her honour,
The proudest of them shall well hear of it.
Time hath not yet so dried this blood of mine,
Nor age so eat up my invention,
Nor fortune made such havoc of my means,
Nor my bad life reft me so much of friends,
But they shall find, awaked in such a kind,
Both strength of limb and policy of mind,
Ability in means and choice of friends,
To quit me of them thoroughly.

FRIAR.   Pause awhile,
And let my counsel sway you in this case.
Your daughter here the princes left for dead:
Let her awhile be secretly kept in,

And publish it that she is dead indeed;
Maintain a mourning ostentation,
And on your family's old monument
Hang mournful epitaphs, and do all rites
That appertain unto a burial.

LEON. What shall become of this? what will this do?

FRIAR. Marry, this, well carried, shall on her behalf
Change slander to remorse; that is some good:
But not for that dream I on this strange course,
But on this travail look for greater birth.
She dying, as it must be so maintain'd,
Upon the instant that she was accused,
Shall be lamented, pitied, and excused
Of every hearer: for it so falls out,
That what we have we prize not to the worth
Whiles we enjoy it; but being lack'd and lost,
Why, then we rack the value, then we find
The virtue that possession would not show us
Whiles it was ours. So will it fare with Claudio:
When he shall hear she died upon his words,
The idea of her life shall sweetly creep
Into his study of imagination;
And every lovely organ of her life
Shall come apparell'd in more precious habit,
More moving-delicate and full of life,
Into the eye and prospect of his soul,
Than when she lived indeed; then shall he mourn,
If ever love had interest in his liver,
And wish he had not so accused her,
No, though he thought his accusation true.
Let this be so, and doubt not but success
Will fashion the event in better shape
Than I can lay it down in likelihood.
But if all aim but this be levell'd false,
The supposition of the lady's death
Will quench the wonder of her infamy:
And if it sort not well, you may conceal her,
As best befits her wounded reputation,

              In some reclusive and religious life,
              Out of all eyes, tongues, minds, and injuries.
BENE.   Signior Leonato, let the friar advise you:
              And though you know my inwardness and love
              Is very much unto the prince and Claudio,
              Yet, by mine honour, I will deal in this
              As secretly and justly as your soul
              Should with your body.
LEON.   Being that I flow in grief,
              The smallest twine may lead me.
FRIAR.   'Tis well consented: presently away;
                  For to strange sores strangely they strain the cure.
              Come, lady, die to live: this wedding-day
                  Perhaps is but prolong'd: have patience and endure.
                                          [*Exeunt all but* BENEDICK *and* BEATRICE.]
BENE.   Lady Beatrice, have you wept all this while?
BEAT.   Yea, and I will weep a while longer.
BENE.   I will not desire that.
BEAT.   You have no reason; I do it freely.
BENE.   Surely I do believe your fair cousin is wronged.
BEAT.   Ah, how much might the man deserve of me that would right
              her!
BENE.   Is there any way to show such friendship?
BEAT.   A very even way, but no such friend.
BENE.   May a man do it?
BEAT.   It is a man's office, but not yours.
BENE.   I do love nothing in the world so well as you: is not that strange?
BEAT.   As strange as the thing I know not. It were as possible for me to
              say I loved nothing so well as you: but believe me not; and yet I lie
              not; I confess nothing, nor I deny nothing. I am sorry for my cousin.
BENE.   By my sword, Beatrice, thou lovest me.
BEAT.   Do not swear, and eat it.
BENE.   I will swear by it that you love me; and I will make him eat it
              that says I love not you.
BEAT.   Will you not eat your word?
BENE.   With no sauce that can be devised to it. I protest I love thee.
BEAT.   Why, then, God forgive me!
BENE.   What offence, sweet Beatrice?

BEAT.   You have stayed me in a happy hour: I was about to protest I
loved you.

BENE.   And do it with all thy heart.

BEAT.   I love you with so much of my heart, that none is left to protest.

BENE.   Come, bid me do any thing for thee.

BEAT.   Kill Claudio.

BENE.   Ha! not for the wide world.

BEAT.   You kill me to deny it. Farewell.

BENE.   Tarry, sweet Beatrice.

BEAT.   I am gone, though I am here: there is no love in you: nay, I pray
you, let me go.

BENE.   Beatrice,—

BEAT.   In faith, I will go.

BENE.   We'll be friends first.

BEAT.   You dare easier be friends with me than fight with mine enemy.

BENE.   Is Claudio thine enemy?

BEAT.   Is he not approved in the height a villain, that hath slandered,
scorned, dishonoured my kinswoman? O that I were a man! What,
bear her in hand until they come to take hands; and then, with
public accusation, uncovered slander, unmitigated rancour,—O
God, that I were a man! I would eat his heart in the market-place.

BENE.   Hear me, Beatrice,—

BEAT.   Talk with a man out at a window! A proper saying!

BENE.   Nay, but, Beatrice,—

BEAT.   Sweet Hero! She is wronged, she is slandered, she is undone.

BENE.   Beat—

BEAT.   Princes and counties! Surely, a princely testimony, a goodly
count, Count Comfect;[2] a sweet gallant, surely! O that I were a
man for his sake! or that I had any friend would be a man for my
sake! But manhood is melted into courtesies, valour into compliment, and men are only turned into tongue, and trim ones too: he
is now as valiant as Hercules that only tells a lie, and swears it. I
cannot be a man with wishing, therefore I will die a woman with
grieving.

BENE.   Tarry, good Beatrice. By this hand, I love thee.

---

2. *Count Comfect*] a sugar-plum count; "comfect" is the same as "comfit," a sweetmeat.

BEAT.   Use it for my love some other way than swearing by it.

BENE.   Think you in your soul the Count Claudio hath wronged Hero?

BEAT.   Yea, as sure as I have a thought or a soul.

BENE.   Enough, I am engaged; I will challenge him. I will kiss your hand, and so I leave you. By this hand, Claudio shall render me a dear account. As you hear of me, so think of me. Go, comfort your cousin: I must say she is dead: and so, farewell.   [*Exeunt.*]

SCENE II. *A prison*.

Enter DOGBERRY, VERGES, *and* Sexton, *in gowns; and the* Watch, *with* CONRADE *and* BORACHIO.

DOG.   Is our whole dissembly[1] appeared?

VERG.   O, a stool and a cushion for the sexton.

SEX.   Which be the malefactors?

DOG.   Marry, that am I and my partner.

VERG.   Nay, that's certain; we have the exhibition to examine.

SEX.   But which are the offenders that are to be examined? let them come before master constable.

DOG.   Yea, marry, let them come before me. What is your name, friend?

BORA.   Borachio.

DOG.   Pray, write down, Borachio. Yours, sirrah?

CON.   I am a gentleman, sir, and my name is Conrade.

DOG.   Write down, master gentleman Conrade. Masters, do you serve God?

CON. ⎫
BORA. ⎭   Yea, sir, we hope.

---

1. *dissembly*] i.e., assembly.

DOG.   Write down, that they hope they serve God: and write God first; for God defend but God should go before such villains! Masters, it is proved already that you are little better than false knaves; and it will go near to be thought so shortly. How answer you for yourselves?

CON.   Marry, sir, we say we are none.

DOG.   A marvellous witty fellow, I assure you; but I will go about with him. Come you hither, sirrah; a word in your ear: sir, I say to you, it is thought you are false knaves.

BORA.   Sir, I say to you we are none.

DOG.   Well, stand aside. 'Fore God, they are both in a tale. Have you writ down, that they are none?

SEX.   Master constable, you go not the way to examine: you must call forth the watch that are their accusers.

DOG.   Yea, marry, that's the eftest[2] way. Let the watch come forth. Masters, I charge you, in the prince's name, accuse these men.

FIRST WATCH.   This man said, sir, that Don John, the prince's brother, was a villain.

DOG.   Write down, Prince John a villain. Why, this is flat perjury, to call a prince's brother villain.

BORA.   Master constable,—

DOG.   Pray thee, fellow, peace: I do not like thy look, I promise thee.

SEX.   What heard you him say else?

SEC. WATCH.   Marry, that he had received a thousand ducats of Don John for accusing the Lady Hero wrongfully.

DOG.   Flat burglary as ever was committed.

VERG.   Yea, by mass, that it is.

SEX.   What else, fellow?

FIRST WATCH.   And that Count Claudio did mean, upon his words, to disgrace Hero before the whole assembly, and not marry her.

DOG.   O villain! thou wilt be condemned into everlasting redemption[3] for this.

SEX.   What else?

WATCH.   This is all.

---

2. *eftest*] the meaning is uncertain; possibly Dogberry's word for easiest.
3. *redemption*] i.e., perdition.

SEX.   And this is more, masters, than you can deny. Prince John is this
       morning secretly stolen away; Hero was in this manner accused, in
       this very manner refused, and upon the grief of this suddenly died.
       Master constable, let these men be bound, and brought to
       Leonato's: I will go before and show him their examination. [*Exit.*]

DOG.   Come, let them be opinioned.[4]

VERG. Let them be in the hands—

CON.   Off, coxcomb!

DOG.   God's my life, where's the sexton? let him write down, the
       prince's officer, coxcomb. Come, bind them. Thou naughty varlet!

CON.   Away! you are an ass, you are an ass.

DOG.   Dost thou not suspect[5] my place? dost thou not suspect my
       years? O that he were here to write me down an ass! But, masters,
       remember that I am an ass; though it be not written down, yet
       forget not that I am an ass. No, thou villain, thou art full of piety,[6] as
       shall be proved upon thee by good witness. I am a wise fellow; and,
       which is more, an officer; and, which is more, a householder; and,
       which is more, as pretty a piece of flesh as any is in Messina; and
       one that knows the law, go to; and a rich fellow enough, go to; and a
       fellow that hath had losses; and one that hath two gowns, and every
       thing handsome about him. Bring him away. O that I had been writ
       down an ass!   [*Exeunt.*]

---

4. *opinioned*] i.e., pinioned.
5. *suspect*] i.e., respect.
6. *piety*] i.e., impiety.

ACT V.

SCENE I. *Before* LEONATO'S *house*.

Enter LEONATO *and* ANTONIO.

ANT. If you go on thus, you will kill yourself;
 And 'tis not wisdom thus to second grief
 Against yourself.
LEON.   I pray thee, cease thy counsel,
 Which falls into mine ears as profitless
 As water in a sieve: give not me counsel;
 Nor let no comforter delight mine ear
 But such a one whose wrongs do suit with mine.
 Bring me a father that so loved his child,
 Whose joy of her is overwhelm'd like mine,
 And bid him speak of patience;
 Measure his woe the length and breadth of mine,
 And let it answer every strain for strain,
 As thus for thus, and such a grief for such,
 In every lineament, branch, shape, and form:
 If such a one will smile, and stroke his beard,
 Bid sorrow wag, cry 'hem!' when he should groan,
 Patch grief with proverbs, make misfortune drunk
 With candle-wasters; bring him yet to me,
 And I of him will gather patience.
 But there is no such man: for, brother, men
 Can counsel and speak comfort to that grief
 Which they themselves not feel; but, tasting it,
 Their counsel turns to passion, which before
 Would give preceptial medicine to rage,

59

Fetter strong madness in a silken thread,
Charm ache with air, and agony with words:
No, no; 'tis all men's office to speak patience
To those that wring under the load of sorrow,
But no man's virtue nor sufficiency,
To be so moral when he shall endure
The like himself. Therefore give me no counsel:
My griefs cry louder than advertisement.

ANT.   Therein do men from children nothing differ.

LEON.   I pray thee, peace. I will be flesh and blood;
For there was never yet philosopher
That could endure the toothache patiently,
However they have writ the style of gods,
And made a push at chance and sufferance.

ANT.   Yet bend not all the harm upon yourself;
Make those that do offend you suffer too.

LEON.   There thou speak'st reason: nay, I will do so.
My soul doth tell me Hero is belied;
And that shall Claudio know; so shall the prince,
And all of them that thus dishonour her.

ANT.   Here comes the prince and Claudio hastily.

Enter DON PEDRO *and* CLAUDIO.

D. PEDRO.   Good den, good den.

CLAUD.   Good day to both of you.

LEON.   Hear you, my lords,—

D. PEDRO.   We have some haste, Leonato.

LEON.   Some haste, my lord! well, fare you well, my lord:
Are you so hasty now? well, all is one.

D. PEDRO.   Nay, do not quarrel with us, good old man.

ANT.   If he could right himself with quarrelling,
Some of us would lie low.

CLAUD.   Who wrongs him?

LEON.   Marry, thou dost wrong me, thou dissembler, thou:—
Nay, never lay thy hand upon thy sword;
I fear thee not.

CLAUD.   Marry, beshrew my hand,
If it should give your age such cause of fear:

In faith, my hand meant nothing to my sword.

LEON.   Tush, tush, man; never fleer and jest at me:
    I speak not like a dotard nor a fool,
    As, under privilege of age, to brag
    What I have done being young, or what would do,
    Were I not old. Know, Claudio, to thy head,
    Thou hast so wrong'd mine innocent child and me,
    That I am forced to lay my reverence by,
    And, with grey hairs and bruise of many days,
    Do challenge thee to trial of a man.
    I say thou hast belied mine innocent child;
    Thy slander hath gone through and through her heart,
    And she lies buried with her ancestors;
    O, in a tomb where never scandal slept,
    Save this of hers, framed by thy villany!

CLAUD.   My villany?

LEON.   Thine, Claudio; thine, I say.

D. PEDRO.   You say not right, old man.

LEON.   My lord, my lord,
    I'll prove it on his body, if he dare,
    Despite his nice fence and his active practice,
    His May of youth and bloom of lustihood.

CLAUD.   Away! I will not have to do with you.

LEON.   Canst thou so daff me? Thou hast kill'd my child:
   If thou kill'st me, boy, thou shalt kill a man.

ANT.   He shall kill two of us, and men indeed:
    But that's no matter; let him kill one first;
    Win me and wear me; let him answer me.
    Come, follow me, boy; come, sir boy, come, follow me:
    Sir boy, I'll whip you from your foining[1] fence;
    Nay, as I am a gentleman, I will.

LEON.   Brother,—

ANT.   Content yourself. God knows I loved my niece;
    And she is dead, slander'd to death by villains,
    That dare as well answer a man indeed

---

1. *foining*] thrusting.

As I dare take a serpent by the tongue:
Boys, apes, braggarts, Jacks, milksops!

LEON.   Brother Antony,—

ANT.   Hold you content. What, man! I know them, yea,
And what they weigh, even to the utmost scruple,—
Scambling, out-facing, fashion-monging boys,
That lie, and cog, and flout, deprave, and slander,
Go antiquely, and show outward hideousness,
And speak off half a dozen dangerous words,
How they might hurt their enemies, if they durst;
And this is all.

LEON.   But, brother Antony,—

ANT.   Come, 'tis no matter:
Do not you meddle; let me deal in this.

D. PEDRO.   Gentlemen both, we will not wake your patience.
My heart is sorry for your daughter's death:
But, on my honour, she was charged with nothing
But what was true, and very full of proof.

LEON.   My lord, my lord,—

D. PEDRO.   I will not hear you.

LEON.   No? Come, brother; away! I will be heard.

ANT.   And shall, or some of us will smart for it.

                                  [*Exeunt* LEONATO *and* ANTONIO.]

D. PEDRO.   See, see; here comes the man we went to seek.

Enter BENEDICK.

CLAUD.   Now, signior, what news?

BENE.   Good day, my lord.

D. PEDRO.   Welcome, signior: you are almost come to part almost a
fray.

CLAUD.   We had like to have had our two noses snapped off with two
old men without teeth.

D. PEDRO.   Leonato and his brother. What thinkest thou? Had we
fought, I doubt we should have been too young for them.

BENE.   In a false quarrel there is no true valour. I came to seek you both.

CLAUD.   We have been up and down to seek thee; for we are high-
proof melancholy, and would fain have it beaten away. Wilt thou
use thy wit?

BENE.   It is in my scabbard: shall I draw it?

D. PEDRO.   Dost thou wear thy wit by thy side?

CLAUD.   Never any did so, though very many have been beside their wit.
I will bid thee draw, as we do the minstrels; draw, to pleasure us.

D. PEDRO.   As I am an honest man, he looks pale. Art thou sick, or
angry?

CLAUD.   What, courage, man! What though care killed a cat, thou hast
mettle enough in thee to kill care.

BENE.   Sir, I shall meet your wit in the career, an you charge it against
me. I pray you choose another subject.

CLAUD.   Nay, then, give him another staff: this last was broke cross.

D. PEDRO.   By this light, he changes more and more: I think he be
angry indeed.

CLAUD.   If he be, he knows how to turn his girdle.

BENE.   Shall I speak a word in your ear?

CLAUD.   God bless me from a challenge!

BENE.   [*Aside to* CLAUDIO] You are a villain; I jest not: I will make it
good how you dare, with what you dare, and when you dare. Do me
right, or I will protest your cowardice. You have killed a sweet lady,
and her death shall fall heavy on you. Let me hear from you.

CLAUD.   Well, I will meet you, so I may have good cheer.

D. PEDRO.   What, a feast, a feast?

CLAUD.   I'faith, I thank him; he hath bid me to a calf's-head and a
capon; the which if I do not carve most curiously, say my knife's
naught. Shall I not find a woodcock too?

BENE.   Sir, your wit ambles well; it goes easily.

D. PEDRO.   I'll tell thee how Beatrice praised thy wit the other day. I
said, thou hadst a fine wit: 'True,' said she, 'a fine little one.' 'No,'
said I, 'a great wit:' 'Right,' says she, 'a great gross one.' 'Nay,' said
I, 'a good wit:' 'Just,' said she, 'it hurts nobody.' 'Nay,' said I, 'the
gentleman is wise:' 'Certain,' said she, 'a wise gentleman.' 'Nay,'
said I, 'he hath the tongues:' 'That I believe,' said she, 'for he
swore a thing to me on Monday night, which he forswore on
Tuesday morning; there's a double tongue; there's two tongues.'
Thus did she, an hour together, trans-shape thy particular virtues:
yet at last she concluded with a sigh, thou wast the properest man
in Italy.

CLAUD.   For the which she wept heartily, and said she cared not.

D. PEDRO.   Yea, that she did; but yet, for all that, an if she did not hate him deadly, she would love him dearly: the old man's daughter told us all.

CLAUD.   All, all; and, moreover, God saw him when he was hid in the garden.

D. PEDRO.   But when shall we set the savage bull's horns on the sensible Benedick's head?

CLAUD.   Yea, and text underneath, 'Here dwells Benedick the married man'?

BENE.   Fare you well, boy: you know my mind. I will leave you now to your gossip-like humour: you break jests as braggarts do their blades, which, God be thanked, hurt not. My lord, for your many courtesies I thank you: I must discontinue your company: your brother the bastard is fled from Messina: you have among you killed a sweet and innocent lady. For my Lord Lackbeard there, he and I shall meet: and till then peace be with him.   [*Exit.*]

D. PEDRO.   He is in earnest.

CLAUD.   In most profound earnest; and, I'll warrant you, for the love of Beatrice.

D. PEDRO.   And hath challenged thee.

CLAUD.   Most sincerely.

D. PEDRO.   What a pretty thing man is when he goes in his doublet and hose, and leaves off his wit!

CLAUD.   He is then a giant to an ape: but then is an ape a doctor to such a man.

D. PEDRO.   But, soft you, let me be: pluck up, my heart, and be sad. Did he not say, my brother was fled?

Enter DOGBERRY, VERGES, *and the* Watch, *with* CONRADE *and* BO-RACHIO.

DOG.   Come, you, sir: if justice cannot tame you, she shall ne'er weigh more reasons in her balance: nay, an you be a cursing hypocrite once, you must be looked to.

D. PEDRO.   How now? two of my brother's men bound! Borachio one!

CLAUD.   Hearken after their offence, my lord.

D. PEDRO.   Officers, what offence have these men done?

DOG.   Marry, sir, they have committed false report; moreover, they have spoken untruths; secondarily, they are slanders; sixth and lastly, they have belied a lady; thirdly, they have verified unjust things; and, to conclude, they are lying knaves.

D. PEDRO.　First, I ask thee what they have done; thirdly, I ask thee what's their offence; sixth and lastly, why they are committed; and, to conclude, what you lay to their charge.

CLAUD.　Rightly reasoned, and in his own division; and, by my troth, there's one meaning well suited.

D. PEDRO.　Who have you offended, masters, that you are thus bound to your answer? this learned constable is too cunning to be understood: what's your offence?

BORA.　Sweet prince, let me go no farther to mine answer: do you hear me, and let this count kill me. I have deceived even your very eyes: what your wisdoms could not discover, these shallow fools have brought to light; who, in the night, overheard me confessing to this man, how Don John your brother incensed me to slander the Lady Hero; how you were brought into the orchard, and saw me court Margaret in Hero's garments: how you disgraced her, when you should marry her: my villany they have upon record; which I had rather seal with my death than repeat over to my shame. The lady is dead upon mine and my master's false accusation; and, briefly, I desire nothing but the reward of a villain.

D. PEDRO.　Runs not this speech like iron through your blood?

CLAUD.　I have drunk poison whiles he utter'd it.

D. PEDRO.　But did my brother set thee on to this?

BORA.　Yea, and paid me richly for the practice of it.

D. PEDRO.　He is composed and framed of treachery:
And fled he is upon this villany.

CLAUD.　Sweet Hero! now thy image doth appear
In the rare semblance that I loved it first.

DOG.　Come, bring away the plaintiffs: by this time our sexton hath reformed[2] Signior Leonato of the matter: and, masters, do not forget to specify, when time and place shall serve, that I am an ass.

VERG.　Here, here comes master Signior Leonato, and the sexton too.

---

2. *reformed*] i.e., informed.

Re-enter LEONATO *and* ANTONIO, *with the* Sexton.

LEON.   Which is the villain? let me see his eyes,
    That, when I note another man like him,
    I may avoid him: which of these is he?
BORA.   If you would know your wronger, look on me.
LEON.   Art thou the slave that with thy breath hast kill'd
    Mine innocent child?
BORA.   Yea, even I alone.
LEON.   No, not so, villain; thou beliest thyself:
    Here stand a pair of honourable men;
    A third is fled, that had a hand in it.
    I thank you, princes, for my daughter's death:
    Record it with your high and worthy deeds:
    'Twas bravely done, if you bethink you of it.
CLAUD.   I know not how to pray your patience;
    Yet I must speak. Choose your revenge yourself;
    Impose me to what penance your invention
    Can lay upon my sin: yet sinn'd I not
    But in mistaking.
D. PEDRO.   By my soul, nor I:
    And yet, to satisfy this good old man,
    I would bend under any heavy weight
    That he'll enjoin me to.
LEON.   I cannot bid you bid my daughter live;
    That were impossible: but, I pray you both,
    Possess[3] the people in Messina here
    How innocent she died; and if your love
    Can labour aught in sad invention,
    Hang her an epitaph upon her tomb,
    And sing it to her bones, sing it to-night:
    To-morrow morning come you to my house;
    And since you could not be my son-in-law,
    Be yet my nephew: my brother hath a daughter,
    Almost the copy of my child that's dead,

---

3. *Possess*] inform.

And she alone is heir to both of us:
Give her the right you should have given her cousin,
And so dies my revenge.

CLAUD.   O noble sir,
Your over-kindness doth wring tears from me!
I do embrace your offer; and dispose
For henceforth of poor Claudio.

LEON.   To-morrow, then, I will expect your coming;
To-night I take my leave. This naughty man
Shall face to face be brought to Margaret,
Who I believe was pack'd in all this wrong,
Hired to it by your brother.

BORA.   No, by my soul, she was not;
Nor knew not what she did when she spoke to me;
But always hath been just and virtuous
In any thing that I do know by her.

DOG.   Moreover, sir, which indeed is not under white and black, this
plaintiff here, the offender, did call me ass: I beseech you, let it be
remembered in his punishment. And also, the watch heard them
talk of one Deformed: they say he wears a key in his ear, and a lock
hanging by it; and borrows money in God's name, the which he
hath used so long and never paid, that now men grow hard-hearted,
and will lend nothing for God's sake: pray you, examine him upon
that point.

LEON.   I thank thee for thy care and honest pains.

DOG.   Your worship speaks like a most thankful and reverend youth;
and I praise God for you.

LEON.   There's for thy pains.

DOG.   God save the foundation!

LEON.   Go, I discharge thee of thy prisoner, and I thank thee.

DOG.   I leave an arrant knave with your worship; which I beseech your
worship to correct yourself, for the example of others. God keep
your worship! I wish your worship well; God restore you to health! I
humbly give you leave to depart; and if a merry meeting may be
wished, God prohibit it! Come, neighbour.

                                        [*Exeunt* DOGBERRY *and* VERGES.]

LEON.   Until to-morrow morning, lords, farewell.

ANT.   Farewell, my lords: we look for you to-morrow.

D. PEDRO.   We will not fail.

CLAUD.   To-night I'll mourn with Hero.

LEON.   [*To the* Watch] Bring you these fellows on. We'll talk with Margaret,

How her acquaintance grew with this lewd fellow.

                                       [*Exeunt, severally.*]

SCENE II. LEONATO'S *garden*.

Enter BENEDICK *and* MARGARET, *meeting*.

BENE.   Pray thee, sweet Mistress Margaret, deserve well at my hands by helping me to the speech of Beatrice.

MARG.   Will you, then, write me a sonnet in praise of my beauty?

BENE.   In so high a style, Margaret, that no man living shall come over it; for, in most comely truth, thou deservest it.

MARG.   To have no man come over me! why, shall I always keep below stairs?

BENE.   Thy wit is as quick as the greyhound's mouth; it catches.

MARG.   And yours as blunt as the fencer's foils, which hit, but hurt not.

BENE.   A most manly wit, Margaret; it will not hurt a woman: and so, I pray thee, call Beatrice: I give thee the bucklers.

MARG.   Give us the swords; we have bucklers of our own.

BENE.   If you use them, Margaret, you must put in the pikes with a vice; and they are dangerous weapons for maids.

MARG.   Well, I will call Beatrice to you, who I think hath legs.

BENE.   And therefore will come.   [*Exit* MARGARET.]

    [*Sings*]   The god of love,
                      That sits above,
           And knows me, and knows me,
              How pitiful I deserve,—

I mean in singing; but in loving, Leander the good swimmer,

Troilus the first employer of pandars, and a whole bookful of these quondam carpet-mongers, whose names yet run smoothly in the even road of a blank verse, why, they were never so truly turned over and over as my poor self in love. Marry, I cannot show it in rhyme; I have tried: I can find out no rhyme to 'lady' but 'baby,' an innocent rhyme; for 'scorn,' 'horn,' a hard rhyme; for 'school,' 'fool,' a babbling rhyme; very ominous endings: no, I was not born under a rhyming planet, nor I cannot woo in festival terms.

Enter BEATRICE.

Sweet Beatrice, wouldst thou come when I called thee?

BEAT.   Yea, signior, and depart when you bid me.

BENE.   O, stay but till then!

BEAT.   'Then' is spoken; fare you well now: and yet, ere I go, let me go with that I came; which is, with knowing what hath passed between you and Claudio.

BENE.   Only foul words; and thereupon I will kiss thee.

BEAT.   Foul words is but foul wind, and foul wind is but foul breath, and foul breath is noisome; therefore I will depart unkissed.

BENE.   Thou has frighted the word out of his right sense, so forcible is thy wit. But I must tell thee plainly, Claudio undergoes my challenge; and either I must shortly hear from him, or I will subscribe him a coward. And, I pray thee now, tell me for which of my bad parts didst thou first fall in love with me?

BEAT.   For them all together; which maintained so politic a state of evil, that they will not admit any good part to intermingle with them. But for which of my good parts did you first suffer love for me?

BENE.   Suffer love,—a good epithet! I do suffer love indeed, for I love thee against my will.

BEAT.   In spite of your heart, I think; alas, poor heart! If you spite it for my sake, I will spite it for yours; for I will never love that which my friend hates.

BENE.   Thou and I are too wise to woo peaceably.

BEAT.   It appears not in this confession: there's not one wise man among twenty that will praise himself.

BENE.   An old, an old instance, Beatrice, that lived in the time of good neighbours. If a man do not erect in this age his own tomb ere he dies, he shall live no longer in monument than the bell rings and the widow weeps.

BEAT.   And how long is that, think you?

BENE.   Question: why, an hour in clamour, and a quarter in rheum: therefore is it most expedient for the wise, if Don Worm, his conscience, find no impediment to the contrary, to be the trumpet of his own virtues, as I am to myself. So much for praising myself, who, I myself will bear witness, is praiseworthy: and now tell me, how doth your cousin?

BEAT.   Very ill.

BENE.   And how do you?

BEAT.   Very ill too.

BENE.   Serve God, love me, and mend. There will I leave you too, for here comes one in haste.

Enter URSULA.

URS.   Madam, you must come to your uncle. Yonder's old coil at home: it is proved my Lady Hero hath been falsely accused, the prince and Claudio mightily abused; and Don John is the author of all, who is fled and gone. Will you come presently?

BEAT.   Will you go hear this news, signior?

BENE.   I will live in thy heart, die in thy lap, and be buried in thy eyes; and moreover I will go with thee to thy uncle's.   [*Exeunt.*]

SCENE III. *A church.*

Enter DON PEDRO, CLAUDIO, *and three or four with tapers.*

CLAUD.   Is this the monument of Leonato?

A LORD.   It is, my lord.

CLAUD.   [*Reading out of a scroll*]

Done to death by slanderous tongues
    Was the Hero that here lies:
Death, in guerdon[1] of her wrongs,
    Gives her fame which never dies.
So the life that died with shame
Lives in death with glorious fame.

Hang thou there upon the tomb,
Praising her when I am dumb.
Now, music, sound, and sing your solemn hymn.

SONG.

Pardon, goddess of the night,
Those that slew thy virgin knight;
For the which, with songs of woe,
Round about her tomb they go.
    Midnight, assist our moan;
    Help us to sigh and groan,
        Heavily, heavily:
    Graves, yawn, and yield your dead,
    Till death be uttered,
        Heavily, heavily.

CLAUD.   Now, unto thy bones good night!
    Yearly will I do this rite.
D. PEDRO.   Good morrow, masters; put your torches out:
    The wolves have prey'd; and look, the gentle day,
    Before the wheels of Phœbus, round about
    Dapples the drowsy east with spots of grey.
    Thanks to you all, and leave us: fare you well.
CLAUD.   Good morrow, masters: each his several way.
D. PEDRO.   Come, let us hence, and put on other weeds;
    And then to Leonato's we will go.
CLAUD.   And Hymen now with luckier issue speed's
    Than this for whom we render'd up this woe.   [Exeunt.]

---

[1] guerdon] reward, recompense.

SCENE IV. *A room in* LEONATO'S *house*.

Enter LEONATO, ANTONIO, BENEDICK, BEATRICE, MARGARET, UR-
    SULA, FRIAR FRANCIS, *and* HERO.

FRIAR.   Did I not tell you she was innocent?
LEON.   So are the prince and Claudio, who accused her
    Upon the error that you heard debated:
    But Margaret was in some fault for this,
    Although against her will, as it appears
    In the true course of all the question.
ANT.   Well, I am glad that all things sort so well.
BENE.   And so am I, being else by faith enforced
    To call young Claudio to a reckoning for it.
LEON.   Well, daughter, and you gentlewomen all,
    Withdraw into a chamber by yourselves,
    And when I send for you, come hither mask'd.

                                          [*Exeunt* Ladies.]

    The prince and Claudio promised by this hour
    To visit me. You know your office, brother:
    You must be father to your brother's daughter,
    And give her to young Claudio.
ANT.   Which I will do with confirm'd countenance.
BENE.   Friar, I must entreat your pains, I think.
FRIAR.   To do what, signior?
BENE.   To bind me, or undo me; one of them.
    Signior Leonato, truth it is, good signior,
    Your niece regards me with an eye of favour.
LEON.   That eye my daughter lent her: 'tis most true.
BENE.   And I do with an eye of love requite her.
LEON.   The sight whereof I think you had from me,
    From Claudio, and the prince: but what's your will?
BENE.   Your answer, sir, is enigmatical:
    But, for my will, my will is, your good will

      May stand with ours, this day to be conjoin'd
      In the state of honourable marriage:
      In which, good friar, I shall desire your help.

LEON.   My heart is with your liking.

FRIAR.   And my help.
      Here comes the prince and Claudio.

Enter DON PEDRO *and* CLAUDIO, *and two or three others.*

D. PEDRO.   Good morrow to this fair assembly.

LEON.   Good morrow, prince; good morrow, Claudio:
      We here attend you. Are you yet determined
      To-day to marry with my brother's daughter?

CLAUD.   I'll hold my mind, were she an Ethiope.

LEON.   Call her forth, brother; here's the friar ready.

                               [*Exit* ANTONIO.]

D. PEDRO.   Good morrow, Benedick. Why, what's the matter,
      That you have such a February face,
      So full of frost, of storm, and cloudiness?

CLAUD.   I think he thinks upon the savage bull.
      Tush, fear not, man; we'll tip thy horns with gold,
      And all Europa shall rejoice at thee;
      As once Europa did at lusty Jove,
      When he would play the noble beast in love.

BENE.   Bull Jove, sir, had an amiable low;
      And some such strange bull leap'd your father's cow,
      And got a calf in that same noble feat
      Much like to you, for you have just his bleat.

CLAUD.   For this I owe you: here comes other reckonings.

Re-enter ANTONIO, *with the* Ladies *masked.*

      Which is the lady I must seize upon?

ANT.   This same is she, and I do give you her.

CLAUD.   Why, then she's mine. Sweet, let me see your face.

LEON.   No, that you shall not, till you take her hand
      Before this friar, and swear to marry her.

CLAUD.   Give me your hand: before this holy friar,
      I am your husband, if you like of me.

HERO.   And when I lived, I was your other wife: [*Unmasking.*]
    And when you loved, you were my other husband.
CLAUD.   Another Hero!
HERO.   Nothing certainer:
    One Hero died defiled; but I do live,
    And surely as I live, I am a maid.
D. PEDRO.   The former Hero! Hero that is dead!
LEON.   She died, my lord, but whiles her slander lived.
FRIAR.   All this amazement can I qualify;
    When after that the holy rites are ended,
    I'll tell you largely of fair Hero's death:
    Meantime let wonder seem familiar,
    And to the chapel let us presently.
BENE.   Soft and fair, friar. Which is Beatrice?
BEAT.   [*Unmasking*] I answer to that name. What is your will?
BENE.   Do not you love me?
BEAT.   Why, no; no more than reason.
BENE.   Why, then your uncle, and the prince, and Claudio
    Have been deceived; they swore you did.
BEAT.   Do not you love me?
BENE.   Troth, no; no more than reason.
BEAT.   Why, then my cousin, Margaret, and Ursula
    Are much deceived; for they did swear you did.
BENE.   They swore that you were almost sick for me.
BEAT.   They swore that you were well-nigh dead for me.
BENE.   'Tis no such matter. Then you do not love me?
BEAT.   No, truly, but in friendly recompence.
LEON.   Come, cousin, I am sure you love the gentleman.
CLAUD.   And I'll be sworn upon't that he loves her;
    For here's a paper, written in his hand,
    A halting sonnet of his own pure brain,
    Fashion'd to Beatrice.
HERO.   And here's another,
    Writ in my cousin's hand, stolen from her pocket,
    Containing her affection unto Benedick.
BENE.   A miracle! here's our own hands against our hearts. Come, I
    will have thee; but, by this light, I take thee for pity.
BEAT.   I would not deny you; but, by this good day, I yield upon great

persuasion; and partly to save your life, for I was told you were in a consumption.

BENE.   Peace! I will stop your mouth.   [*Kissing her.*]

D. PEDRO.   How dost thou, Benedick, the married man?

BENE.   I'll tell thee what, prince; a college of wit-crackers cannot flout me out of my humour. Dost thou think I care for a satire or an epigram? No: if a man will be beaten with brains, a' shall wear nothing handsome about him. In brief, since I do purpose to marry, I will think nothing to any purpose that the world can say against it; and therefore never flout at me for what I have said against it; for man is a giddy thing, and this is my conclusion. For thy part, Claudio, I did think to have beaten thee; but in that thou art like to be my kinsman, live unbruised, and love my cousin.

CLAUD.   I had well hoped thou wouldst have denied Beatrice, that I might have cudgelled thee out of thy single life, to make thee a double-dealer; which, out of question, thou wilt be, if my cousin do not look exceeding narrowly to thee.

BENE.   Come, come, we are friends: let's have a dance ere we are married, that we may lighten our own hearts, and our wives' heels.

LEON.   We'll have dancing afterward.

BENE.   First, of my word; therefore play, music. Prince, thou art sad; get thee a wife, get thee a wife: there is no staff more reverend than one tipped with horn.

Enter a Messenger.

MESS.   My lord, your brother John is ta'en in flight,
And brought with armed men back to Messina.

BENE.   Think not on him till to-morrow: I'll devise thee brave punishments for him. Strike up, pipers.   [*Dance.*]
[*Exeunt.*]

Study Guide

Text by
Louva Elizabeth Irvine
(M.A., New York Institute of Technology)

Learning-to-Read-Through-the-Arts Instructor
Solomon R. Guggenheim Museum
New York City, New York

Contents

**Each Scene includes List of Characters,
Summary, Analysis, Study Questions and
Answers, and Suggested Essay Topics.**

SECTION ONE

Introduction

The Life and Work of William Shakespeare

The details of William Shakespeare's life are sketchy, mostly mere surmise based upon court or other clerical records. His parents, John and Mary (Arden), were married about 1557; she was of the landed gentry, and he was a yeoman—a glover and commodities merchant. By 1568, John had risen through the ranks of town government and held the position of high bailiff, which was a position similar to mayor. William, the eldest son and the third of eight children, was born in 1564, probably on April 23, several days before his baptism on April 26 in Stratford-upon-Avon. Shakespeare is also believed to have died on the same date—April 23—in 1616.

It is believed that William attended the local grammar school in Stratford where his parents lived, and that he studied primarily Latin, rhetoric, logic, and literature. Shakespeare probably left school at age 15, which was the norm, to take a job, especially since this was the period of his father's financial difficulty. At age 18 (1582), William married Anne Hathaway, a local farmer's daughter who was eight years his senior. Their first daughter (Susanna) was born six months later (1583), and twins Judith and Hamnet were born in 1585.

Shakespeare's life can be divided into three periods: the first 20 years in Stratford, which include his schooling, early marriage, and fatherhood; the next 25 years as an actor and playwright in London; and the last five in retirement in Stratford where he enjoyed moderate wealth gained from his theatrical successes. The years linking the first two periods are marked by a lack of information about Shakespeare, and are often referred to as the "dark years."

At some point during the "dark years," Shakespeare began his career with a London theatrical company, perhaps in 1589, for he was already an actor and playwright of some note by 1592. Shakespeare apparently wrote and acted for numerous theatrical companies, including Pembroke's Men, and Strange's Men, which later became the Chamberlain's Men, with whom he remained for the rest of his career.

In 1592, the Plague closed the theaters for about two years, and Shakespeare turned to writing book-length narrative poetry. Most notable were *Venus and Adonis* and *The Rape of Lucrece*, both of which were dedicated to the Earl of Southampton, whom scholars accept as Shakespeare's friend and benefactor despite a lack of documentation. During this same period, Shakespeare was writing his sonnets, which are more likely signs of the time's fashion rather than actual love poems detailing any particular relationship. He returned to playwriting when theaters reopened in 1594, and did not continue to write poetry. His sonnets were published without his consent in 1609, shortly before his retirement.

Amid all of his success, Shakespeare suffered the loss of his only son, Hamnet, who died in 1596 at the age of 11. But Shakespeare's career continued unabated, and in London in 1599, he became one of the partners in the new Globe Theater, which was built by the Chamberlain's Men.

Shakespeare wrote very little after 1612, which was the year he completed *Henry VIII*. It was during a performance of this play in 1613 that the Globe caught fire and burned to the ground. Sometime between 1610 and 1613, Shakespeare returned to Stratford, where he owned a large house and property, to spend his remaining years with his family.

William Shakespeare died on April 23, 1616, and was buried two days later in the chancel of Holy Trinity Church, where he had been baptized exactly 52 years earlier. His literary legacy included 37 plays, 154 sonnets, and five major poems.

Incredibly, most of Shakespeare's plays had never been published in anything except pamphlet form, and were simply extant as acting scripts stored at the Globe. Theater scripts were not regarded as literary works of art, but only the basis for the performance. Plays were simply a popular form of entertainment for all layers of society in Shakespeare's time. Only the efforts of two of Shakespeare's company, John Heminges and Henry Condell, preserved his 36 plays (minus *Pericles*, the thirty-seventh).

Shakespeare's Language

Shakespeare's language can create a strong pang of intimidation, even fear, in a large number of modern-day readers. Fortunately, however, this need not be the case. All that is needed to master the art of reading Shakespeare is to practice the techniques of unraveling uncommonly-structured sentences and to become familiar with the poetic use of uncommon words. We must realize that during the 400-year span between Shakespeare's time and our own, both the way we live and speak has changed. Although most of his vocabulary is in use today, some of it is obsolete, and what may be most confusing is that some of his words are used today, but with slightly different or totally different meanings. On the stage, actors readily dissolve these language stumbling blocks. They study Shakespeare's dialogue and express it dramatically in word and in action so that its meaning is graphically enacted. If the reader studies Shakespeare's lines as an actor does, looking up and reflecting upon the meaning of unfamiliar words until real voice is discovered, he or she will suddenly experience the excitement, the depth, and the sheer poetry of what these characters say.

Shakespeare's Sentences

In English, or any other language, the meaning of a sentence greatly depends upon where each word is placed in that sentence. "The child hurt the mother" and "The mother hurt the child" have opposite meanings, even though the words are the same, simply because the words are arranged differently. Because word position is so integral to English, the reader will find unfamiliar word arrangements confusing, even difficult to understand. Since Shakespeare's plays are poetic dramas, he often shifts from average word arrangements to the strikingly unusual so that the line will conform to the desired poetic rhythm. Often, too, Shakespeare employs unusual word order to afford a character his own specific style of speaking.

Today, English sentence structure follows a sequence of subject first, verb second, and an optional object third. Shakespeare, however, often places the verb before the subject, which reads, "Speaks he" rather than "He speaks." Solanio speaks with this inverted structure in *The Merchant of Venice* stating, "I should be still/Plucking the grass to know where sits the wind" (Bevington edition, I, i, ll.17-19), while today's standard English word order would have the clause at the end of this line read, "where the wind sits." "Wind" is the subject of this clause, and "sits" is the verb. Bassanio's words in Act Two also exemplify this inversion: "And in such eyes as ours appear not faults" (II, ii, l. 184). In our normal word order, we would say, "Faults do not appear in eyes such as ours," with "faults" as the subject in both Shakespeare's word order and ours.

Inversions like these are not troublesome, but when Shakespeare positions the predicate adjective or the object before the subject and verb, we are sometimes surprised. For example, rather than "I saw him," Shakespeare may use a structure such as "Him I saw." Similarly, "Cold the morning is" would be used for our "The morning is cold." Lady Macbeth demonstrates this inversion as she speaks of her husband: "Glamis thou art, and Cawdor, and shalt be/What thou art promised" (Macbeth, I, v, ll. 14-15). In current English word order, this quote would begin, "Thou art Glamis, and Cawdor."

In addition to inversions, Shakespeare purposefully keeps words apart that we generally keep together. To illustrate, consider Bassanio's humble admission in *The Merchant of Venice*: "I owe you much, and, like a wilful youth,/That which I owe is lost" (I, i, ll. 146-147). The phrase, "like a wilful youth," separates the regular sequence of "I owe you much" and "That which I owe is lost." To understand more clearly this type of passage, the reader could rearrange these word groups into our conventional order: I owe you much and I wasted what you gave me because I was young and impulsive. While these rearranged clauses will sound like normal English and will be simpler to understand, they will no longer have the desired poetic rhythm, and the emphasis will now be on the wrong words.

As we read Shakespeare, we will find words that are separated by long, interruptive statements. Often subjects are separated from verbs, and verbs are separated from objects. These long interruptions can be used to give a character dimension or to add an element of suspense. For example, in *Romeo and Juliet* Benvolio describes both Romeo's moodiness and his own sensitive and thoughtful nature:

> I, measuring his affections by my own,
> Which then most sought, where most might not be found,
> Being one too many by my weary self,
> Pursu'd my humour, not pursuing his,
> And gladly shunn'd who gladly fled from me.
> (I i, ll 126-130)

In this passage, the subject "I" is distanced from its verb "Pursu'd." The long interruption serves to provide information which is integral to the plot. Another example, taken from *Hamlet*, is the ghost, Hamlet's father, who describes Hamlet's uncle, Claudius, as

> ...that incestuous, that adulterate beast,
> With witchcraft of his wit, with traitorous gifts—
> O wicked wit and gifts, that have the power
> So to seduce—won to his shameful lust
> The will of my most seeming virtuous queen.
> (I, v, ll. 43-47)

From this we learn that Prince Hamlet's mother is the victim of an evil seduction and deception. The delay between the subject, "beast," and the verb, "won," creates a moment of tension filled with the image of a cunning predator waiting for the right moment to spring into attack. This interruptive passage allows the play to unfold crucial information and thus to build the tension necessary to produce a riveting drama.

While at times these long delays are merely for decorative purposes, they are often used to narrate a particular situation or to enhance character development. As *Antony and Cleopatra* opens, an interruptive passage occurs in the first few lines. Although the delay is not lengthy, Philo's words vividly portray Antony's military prowess while they also reveal the immediate concern of the drama. Antony is distracted from his career and is now focused on Cleopatra:

> ...those goodly eyes,
> That o'er the files and musters of the war
> Have glow'd like plated Mars, now bend, now turn
> The office and devotion of their view
> Upon a tawny front.... (I, i, ll. 2-6)

Whereas Shakespeare sometimes heaps detail upon detail, his sentences are often elliptical, that is, they omit words we expect in written English sentences. In fact, we often do this in our spoken conversations. For instance, we say, "You see that?" when we really mean, "Did you see that?" Reading poetry or listening to lyrics in music conditions us to supply the omitted words, and it makes us more comfortable reading this type of dialogue. Consider one passage in *The Merchant of Venice* where Antonio's friends ask him why he seems so sad and Solanio tells Antonio, "Why, then you are in love" (I, i, l. 46). When Antonio denies this, Solanio responds, "Not in love neither?" (I, i, l. 47). The word "you" is omitted but understood despite the confusing double negative.

In addition to leaving out words, Shakespeare often uses intentionally vague language, a strategy which taxes the reader's attentiveness. In *Antony and Cleopatra*, Cleopatra, upset that Antony is leaving for Rome after learning that his wife died in battle, convinces him to stay in Egypt:

> Sir, you and I must part, but that's not it:
> Sir you and I have lov'd, but there's not it;
> That you know well, something it is I would—
> O, my oblivion is a very Antony,
> And I am all forgotten, (I, iii, ll. 87-91, emphasis added)

In line 89, "...something it is I would" suggests that there is something that she would want to say, do, or have done. The intentional vagueness leaves us, and certainly Antony, to wonder.

Though this sort of writing may appear lackadaisical for all that it leaves out, here the vagueness functions to portray Cleopatra as rhetorically sophisticated. Similarly, when asked what thing a crocodile is (meaning Antony himself who is being compared to a crocodile), Antony slyly evades the question by giving a vague reply:

> It is shap'd, sir, like itself, and it is as broad as it hath breadth. It is just so high as it is, and moves with it own organs. It lives by that which nourisheth it, and, the elements once out of it, it transmigrates.
> (II, vii, ll. 43-46)

This kind of evasiveness, or double-talk, occurs often in Shakespeare's writing and requires extra patience on the part of the reader.

Shakespeare's Words

As we read Shakespeare's plays, we will encounter uncommon words. Many of these words are not in use today. As *Romeo and Juliet* opens, we notice words like "shrift" (confession) and "holidame" (a holy relic). Words like these should be explained in notes to the text. Shakespeare also employs words which we still use, though with different meaning. For example, in *The Merchant of Venice* "caskets" refer to small, decorative chests for holding jewels. However, modern readers may think of a large cask instead of the smaller, diminutive casket.

Another trouble modern readers will have with Shakespeare's English is with words that are still in use today, but which mean something different in Elizabethan use. In *The Merchant of Venice*, Shakespeare uses the word "straight" (as in "straight away") where we would say "immediately." Here, the modern reader is unlikely to carry away the wrong message, however, since the modern meaning will simply make no sense. In this case, textual notes will clarify a phrase's meaning. To cite another example, in *Romeo and Juliet*, after Mercutio dies, Romeo states that the "black fate on moe days doth depend" (emphasis added). In this case, "depend" really means "impend."

Shakespeare's Wordplay

All of Shakespeare's works exhibit his mastery of playing with language and with such variety that many people have authored entire books on this subject alone. Shakespeare's most frequently used types of wordplay are common: metaphors, similes, synecdoche and metonymy, personification, allusion, and puns. It is when Shakespeare violates the normal use of these devices, or rhetorical figures, that the language becomes confusing.

A metaphor is a comparison in which an object or idea is replaced by another object or idea with common attributes. For example, in *Macbeth* a murderer tells Macbeth that Banquo has been murdered, as directed, but that his son, Fleance, escaped, having witnessed his father's murder. Fleance, now a threat to Macbeth, is described as a serpent:

> There the grown serpent lies, the worm that's fled
> Hath nature that in time will venom breed,
> No teeth for the present. (III, iv, ll. 29-31, emphasis added)

Similes, on the other hand, compare objects or ideas while using the words "like" or "as." In *Romeo and Juliet*, Romeo tells Juliet that "Love goes toward love as schoolboys from their books" (II, ii, l. 156). Such similes often give way to more involved comparisons, "extended similes." For example, Juliet tells Romeo:

> 'Tis almost morning, I would have thee gone
> That lets it hop a little from his hand
> Like a poor prisoner in his twisted gyves,
> And with silken thread plucks it back again,
> So loving-jealous of his liberty.
> (II, ii, ll. 176-181, emphasis added)

An epic simile, a device borrowed from heroic poetry, is an extended simile that builds into an even more elaborate comparison. In *Macbeth*, Macbeth describes King Duncan's virtues with an angelic, celestial simile and then drives immediately into another simile that redirects us into a vision of warfare and destruction:

> ...Besides this Duncan
> Hath borne his faculties so meek, hath been
> So clear in his great office, that his virtues
> Will plead like angels, trumpet-tongued, against
> The deep damnation of his taking-off;
> And pity, like a naked new-born babe,
> Striding the blast, or heaven's cherubim, horsed
> Upon the sightless couriers of the air,
> Shall blow the horrid deed in every eye,
> That tears shall drown the wind....
> (I, vii, ll. 16-25, emphasis added)

Shakespeare employs other devices, like synecdoche and metonymy, to achieve "verbal economy," or using one or two words to express more than one thought. Synecdoche is a figure of speech using a part for the whole. An example of synecdoche is using the word "boards" to imply a stage. Boards are only a small part of the materials that make up a stage; however, the term boards has become a colloquial synonym for stage. Metonymy is a figure of speech using the name of one thing for that of another which it is associated. An example of metonymy is using "crown" to mean the king (as used in the sentence "These lands belong to the crown"). Since a crown is associated with or an attribute of the king, the word "crown" has become a metonymy for the king. It is important to understand that every metonymy is a synecdoche, but not every synecdoche is a metonymy. This rule is true because a metonymy must not only be a part of the root word, making a synecdoche, but also be a unique attribute of or associated with the root word.

Synecdoche and metonymy in Shakespeare's works is often very confusing to a new student because he creates uses for words that they usually do not perform. This technique is often complicated and yet very subtle, which makes it difficult for a new student to dissect and understand. An example of these devices in one of Shakespeare's plays can be found in *The Merchant of Venice*. In warning his daughter, Jessica, to ignore the Christian revelries in the streets below, Shylock says:

Lock up my doors; and when you hear the drum
And the vile squealing of the wry-necked fife,
Clamber not you up to the casements then…"
(I, v, ll. 30-32)

The phrase of importance in this quote is "the wry-necked fife." When a reader examines this phrase it does not seem to make sense; a fife is a cylinder-shaped instrument, there is no part of it that can be called a neck. The phrase then must be taken to refer to the fife-player, who has to twist his or her neck to play the fife. Fife, therefore, is a synecdoche for fife-player, much as boards is for stage. The trouble with understanding this phrase is that "vile squealing" logically refers to the sound of the fife, not the fife-player, and the reader might be led to take fife as the instrument because of the parallel reference to "drum" in the previous line. The best solution to this quandary is that Shakespeare uses the word "fife" to refer to both the instrument and the player. Both the player and the instrument are needed to complete the wordplay in this phrase, which, though difficult to understand to new readers, cannot be seen as a flaw since Shakespeare manages to convey two meanings with one word. This remarkable example of synecdoche illuminates Shakespeare's mastery of "verbal economy."

Shakespeare also uses vivid and imagistic wordplay through personification, in which human capacities and behaviors are attributed to inanimate objects. Bassanio, in *The Merchant of Venice*, almost speechless when Portia promises to marry him and share all her worldly wealth, states "my blood speaks to you in my veins…" (III, ii, l. 176). How deeply he must feel since even his blood can speak. Similarly, Portia, learning of the penalty that Antonio must pay for defaulting on his debt, tells Salerio, "There are some shrewd contents in yond same paper/That steals the color from Bassanio's cheek" (III, ii, ll. 243-244).

Another important facet of Shakespeare's rhetorical repertoire is his use of allusion. An allusion is a reference to another author or to an historical figure or event. Very often Shakespeare alludes to the heroes and heroines of Ovid's *Metamorphoses*. For example, in Cymbeline an entire room is decorated with images

illustrating the stories from this classical work, and the hero-
ine, Imogen, has been reading from this text. Similarly, in *Titus
Andronicus* characters not only read directly from the *Metamorphoses*, but a subplot re-enacts one of the *Metamorphoses's* most
famous stories, the rape and mutilation of Philomel.

Another way Shakespeare uses allusion is to drop names
of mythological, historical, and literary figures. In *The Taming
of the Shrew*, for instance, Petruchio compares Katharina, the
woman whom he is courting, to Diana (II, i, l. 55), the virgin goddess, in order to suggest that Katharina is a man-hater. At times,
Shakespeare will allude to well-known figures without so much
as mentioning their names. In *Twelfth Night*, for example, though
the Duke and Valentine are ostensibly interested in Olivia, a rich
countess, Shakespeare asks his audience to compare the Duke's
emotional turmoil to the plight of Acteon, whom the goddess
Diana transforms into a deer to be hunted and killed by Acteon's
own dogs:

Duke: That instant was I turn'd into a hart,
            And my desires, like fell and cruel hounds,
            E'er since pursue me.
            [...]
Valentine: But like a cloistress she will veiled walk,
            And water once a day her chamber round....
            (I, i, l. 20 ff.)

Shakespeare's use of puns spotlights his exceptional wit. His
comedies in particular are loaded with puns, usually of a sexual
nature. Puns work through the ambiguity that results when mul-
tiple senses of a word are evoked; homophones often cause this
sort of ambiguity. In *Antony and Cleopatra*, Enobarbus believes
"there is mettle in death" (I, ii, l. 146), meaning that there is "courage" in death; at the same time, mettle suggests the homophone
metal, referring to swords made of metal causing death. In early
editions of Shakespeare's work there was no distinction made
between the two words. Antony puns on the word "earing," (I,
ii, ll. 112-114) meaning both plowing (as in rooting out weeds)
and hearing: he angrily sends away a messenger, not wishing to
hear the message from his wife, Fulvia: "...O then we bring forth

weeds,/when our quick minds lie still, and our ills told us/Is as our earing." If ill-natured news is planted in one's "hearing," it will render an "earing" (harvest) of ill-natured thoughts. A particularly clever pun, also in *Antony and Cleopatra*, stands out after Antony's troops have fought Octavius's men in Egypt: "We have beat him to his camp. Run one before,/And let the queen know of our gests" (IV, viii, ll. 1-2). Here "gests" means deeds (in this case, deeds of battle); it is also a pun on "guests," as though Octavius's slain soldiers were to be guests when buried in Egypt.

One should note that Elizabethan pronunciation was in several cases different from our own. Thus, modern readers, especially Americans, will miss out on the many puns based on homophones. The textual notes will point out many of these "lost" puns, however.

Shakespeare's sexual innuendoes can be either clever or tedious depending upon the speaker and situation. The modern reader should recall that sexuality in Shakespeare's time was far more complex than in ours and that characters may refer to such things as masturbation and homosexual activity. Textual notes in some editions will point out these puns but rarely explain them. An example of a sexual pun or innuendo can be found in *The Merchant of Venice* when Portia and Nerissa are discussing Portia's past suitors using innuendo to tell of their sexual prowess:

Portia: I pray thee, overname them, and as thou
            namest them, I will describe them, and
            according to my description level at my
            affection.
Nerissa: First, there is the Neapolitan prince.
Portia: Ay, that's a colt indeed, for he doth nothing
            but talk of his horse, and he makes it a great
            appropriation to his own good parts that he can
            shoe him himself. I am much afeard my lady his
            mother played false with the smith.
            (I, ii, ll. 35-45)

The "Neapolitan prince" is given a grade of an inexperienced youth when Portia describes him as a "colt." The prince is thought to be inexperienced because he did nothing but "talk of his horse" (a pun for his penis) and his other great attributes. Portia goes on to say that the prince boasted that he could "shoe him [his horse] himself," a possible pun meaning that the prince was very proud that he could masturbate. Finally, Portia makes an attack upon the prince's mother, saying that "my lady his mother played false with the smith," a pun to say his mother must have committed adultery with a blacksmith to give birth to such a vulgar man having an obsession with "shoeing his horse."

It is worth mentioning that Shakespeare gives the reader hints when his characters might be using puns and innuendoes. In *The Merchant of Venice*, Portia's lines are given in prose when she is joking, or engaged in bawdy conversations. Later on the reader will notice that Portia's lines are rhymed in poetry, such as when she is talking in court or to Bassanio. This is Shakespeare's way of letting the reader know when Portia is jesting and when she is serious.

Shakespeare's Dramatic Verse

Finally, the reader will notice that some lines are actually rhymed verse while others are in verse without rhyme; and much of Shakespeare's drama is in prose. Shakespeare usually has his lovers speak in the language of love poetry which uses rhymed couplets. The archetypal example of this comes, of course, from *Romeo and Juliet*:

> The grey-ey'd morn smiles on the frowning night,
> Check'ring the eastern clouds with streaks of light,
> And fleckled darkness like a drunkard reels
> From forth day's path and Titan's fiery wheels.
> (II, iii, ll. 1-4)

Here it is ironic that Friar Lawrence should speak these lines since he is not the one in love. He, therefore, appears buffoonish and out of touch with reality. Shakespeare often has his characters speak in rhymed verse to let the reader know that the character is acting in jest, and vice-versa.

Perhaps the majority of Shakespeare's lines are in blank verse, a form of poetry which does not use rhyme (hence the name blank) but still employs a rhythm native to the English language, iambic pentameter, where every second syllable in a line of ten syllables receives stress. Consider the following verses from *Hamlet*, and note the accents and the lack of end-rhyme:

> The síngle ánd pecúliar lífe is bóund
> With áll the stréngth and ármor óf the mínd
> (III, iii, ll. 12-13)

The final syllable of these verses receives stress and is said to have a hard, or "strong," ending. A soft ending, also said to be "weak," receives no stress. In *The Tempest*, Shakespeare uses a soft ending to shape a verse that demonstrates through both sound (meter) and sense the capacity of the feminine to propagate:

> and thén I lóv'd thee
> And shów'd thee áll the quálitíes o' th' ísle,
> The frésh spríngs, bríne-pits, bárren pláce and fértile.
> (I, ii, ll. 338-40)

The first and third of these lines here have soft endings.

In general, Shakespeare saves blank verse for his characters of noble birth. Therefore, it is significant when his lofty characters speak in prose. Prose holds a special place in Shakespeare's dialogues; he uses it to represent the speech habits of the common people. Not only do lowly servants and common citizens speak in prose, but important, lower class figures also use this fun, at times ribald variety of speech. Though Shakespeare crafts some very ornate lines in verse, his prose can be equally daunting, for some of his characters may speechify and break into doubletalk in their attempts to show sophistication. A clever instance of this comes when the Third Citizen in *Coriolanus* refers to the people's paradoxical lack of power when they must elect Coriolanus as their new leader once Coriolanus has orated how he has courageously fought for them in battle:

> We have power in ourselves to do it, but it is a
> power that we have no power to do; for if he show us his
> wounds and tell us his deeds, we are to put our tongues
> into those wounds and speak for them; so, if he tell us his
> noble deeds, we must also tell him our noble acceptance

of them. Ingratitude is monstrous, and for the multitude to be ingrateful were to make a monster of the multitude, of the which we, being members, should bring ourselves to be monstrous members.
(II, ii, ll. 3-13)

Notice that this passage contains as many metaphors, hideous though they be, as any other passage in Shakespeare's dramatic verse.

When reading Shakespeare, paying attention to characters who suddenly break into rhymed verse, or who slip into prose after speaking in blank verse, will heighten your awareness of a character's mood and personal development. For instance, in *Antony and Cleopatra*, the famous military leader Marcus Antony usually speaks in blank verse, but also speaks in fits of prose (II, iii, ll. 43-46) once his masculinity and authority have been questioned. Similarly, in *Timon of Athens*, after the wealthy Lord Timon abandons the city of Athens to live in a cave, he harangues anyone whom he encounters in prose (IV, iii, l. 331 ff.). In contrast, the reader should wonder why the bestial Caliban in *The Tempest* speaks in blank verse rather than in prose.

Implied Stage Action

When we read a Shakespearean play, we are reading a performance text. Actors interact through dialogue, but at the same time these actors cry, gesticulate, throw tantrums, pick up daggers, and compulsively wash murderous "blood" from their hands. Some of the action that takes place on stage is explicitly stated in stage directions. However, some of the stage activity is couched within the dialogue itself. Attentiveness to these cues is important as one conceives how to visualize the action. When Iago in *Othello* feigns concern for Cassio whom he himself has stabbed, he calls to the surrounding men, "Come, come:/Lend me a light" (V, i, ll. 86-87). It is almost sure that one of the actors involved will bring him a torch or lantern. In the same play, Emilia, Desdemona's maidservant, asks if she should fetch her lady's nightgown and Desdemona replies, "No, unpin me here" (IV, iii, l. 37). In *Macbeth*, after killing Duncan, Macbeth brings the murder weapon back with him. When he tells his wife that he cannot return to the scene and place the daggers to suggest that the king's guards murdered Duncan, she castigates him: "Infirm of purpose/Give me the daggers. The sleeping and the dead are but as pictures" (II, ii, ll. 50-52). As she exits, it is easy to visualize Lady Macbeth grabbing the daggers from her husband.

For 400 years, readers have found it greatly satisfying to work with all aspects of Shakespeare's language—the implied stage action, word choice, sentence structure, and wordplay—until all aspects come to life. Just as seeing a fine performance of a Shakespearean play is exciting, staging the play in one's own mind's eye, and revisiting lines to enrich the sense of the action, will enhance one's appreciation of Shakespeare's extraordinary literary and dramatic achievements.

Historical Background

The Commedie of much A doo about nothing a booke was entered in the Stationer's Register, the official record book of the London Company of Stationers (booksellers and printers), on August 4, 1600 as a play of *My lord chamberlens men* (Shakespeare's acting company) and stayed (not published) without further permission, to prevent unauthorized publication of this very popular play. This quarto text, generally regarded as having been set from Shakespeare's own manuscript, was the copy used for the First Folio of 1623, which is lightly annotated, with minimal and mostly typographic emendation. Since Will Kempe, the great comic actor who played Dogberry, left the Chamberlain's Men in 1599, it is generally agreed that Shakespeare completed this play no later than 1598–1599. Although scholars have attempted to trace the play's roots to Ariosto's tragedy, *Orlando Furioso*, to Bandello's twenty-second story from the *Novelle*, or to Spenser's poetic work, *The Fairie Queen*, in truth, no play ever existed quite like this one, with its interwoven plots, the wit and verve of Benedick and Beatrice, and the highly inventive comic element of Dogberry and his watch, which gives the Claudio–Hero plot most of its vitality. *Much Ado About Nothing* is a subtler version of *Taming of the Shrew*, transposed from farce to high comedy, and it is the scaffolding upon which *Othello* is built.

Well known and often presented to packed houses before its publication, *Much Ado About Nothing* has not lacked the interest of either producers or reviewers over the last four centuries—it has been popular onstage throughout virtually all of its history. It was performed at court in 1613 for Princess Elizabeth and Frederick, Elector Palantine. David Garrick gave *Much Ado About Nothing* its first performance at Drury Lane on November 14, 1748, playing Benedick brilliantly, and regularly offered it until his farewell performance from the stage in May 9, 1776. Notable presentations in the nineteenth century, when productions tended toward lavish spectacle, include Miss Helen Faucit's personation of Beatrice, noted in the *Manchester Courier* of May 9, 1846 as "a performance of rare beauty" and Henry Irving's "exquisite performance" of Benedick at the Lyceum Theater, noted as having been "given with infinite grace" in the *Saturday Review* of October 21, 1882. Twentieth century renditions have frequently changed the time and locale of the play, with productions as diverse as the American Southwest shoot–em up era, the bicycle–riding Edwardian era and the Teddy Roosevelt era of gramophones and keystone cops. The success of these productions show that the original text is universal enough in appeal and balanced in its composition to withstand these chameleon–like experiments without losing any of its sense.

A. C. Swinburne describes this play as Shakespeare's "most perfect comic masterpiece," and states that "[f]or absolute power of composition, for faultless balance and blameless rectitude of design, there is unquestionably no creation of his hand that will bear comparison with *Much Ado About Nothing*." George Bernard Shaw, on the other hand, while stating that the success of this play "depends on the way it is handled in performance," salutes the Bard as a "great musician" and declares the play "irresistible as poetry" but questions Shakespeare's mastery of "gallant badinage" and dismisses Benedick's wit as "coarse sallies" and Beatrice's wit as "indelicacy," all of which is perhaps more a reflection of the taste of his Victorian time than a true assessment of the play. In the end, the merit of this play rests with its proven ability to continue to touch the hearts and cheer the souls of its audience.

INTRODUCTION

Master List of Characters

Don Pedro—*Prince of Aragon, courtly and conventional. Fearful of his reputation, he is easily duped by his brother's deception. He enjoys matchmaking.*

Leonato—*Governor of Messina and father of Hero, whose conventionality is tested by the depth of his grief.*

Antonio—*Leonato's older brother, who tries to philosophize his brother out of his grief, only to find his own anger stirred.*

Benedick—*Brave, quick-witted and spirited young lord of Padua and a professed misogynist, who will prove his love for Beatrice in a most serious manner.*

Beatrice—*Leonato's niece, whose spirited and merry wit is more than a match for Benedick, and who will, in the end, accept his love and marry him.*

Claudio—*Young lord of Florence, who, easily swayed by outer appearances, revengefully denounces Hero as a wanton on their wedding day.*

Hero—*Leonato's daughter, a chaste and docile maiden, wronged by Don John's slander.*

Margaret and Ursula—*Both gentlewomen attending Hero, Margaret is unwittingly employed in Don John's plot to slander Hero.*

Don John—*Don Pedro's illegitimate brother, an envious and mischief-making malcontent and author of the slander against Hero.*

Borachio and Conrade—*Followers of Don John who assist him in his slander, Borachio is a drunkard.*

Dogberry—*Illiterate master constable, whose love of high-faluting words is only matched by his misuse of them, exposes the slanderous deception, thereby saving Hero.*

Verges—*Headborough, or parish constable, Dogberry's elderly companion.*

Sexton (Francis Seacoal)—*Learned town clerk, recorder of the examination of Conrade and Borachio, who will see past*

Dogberry's bumbling and alert Leonato that his daughter's slanderer has been apprehended.

First Watchman and Second Watchman (George Seacoal)— *Dogberry's assistants, who providentially overhear Borachio describe the details of the deception perpetrated upon Hero.*

Balthasar—*Singer attending Don Pedro, whose out-of-key love song sets the tone of the play.*

Friar Francis—*Priest at the nuptials of Claudio and Hero, who devises a plan to change the hearts of Claudio and Don Pedro and reverse the effects of the slander perpetrated by Don John.*

Messenger to Leonato—*Announcer of the arrival of Don Pedro and his companions.*

Another Messenger—*Calls Leonato to the wedding; alerts Leonato that Don John has been taken.*

Attendants, Musicians, Members of the Watch, Antonio's Son and Other Kinsmen—*Members of the community.*

Summary of the Play

The play is set in and near the house of Leonato, governor of Messina, Sicily. Prince Don Pedro of Aragon with his favorite, Claudio, and Benedick, young cavalier of Padua, as well as Don John, the bastard brother of Don Pedro, come to Leonato's. Claudio instantly falls in love with Hero (her name means chaste), Leonato's only child, whom Don Pedro formally obtains for him. While they wait for the wedding day, they amuse themselves by gulling Benedick and Beatrice (Leonato's niece), verbal adversaries who share a merry wit and a contempt for conventional love, into believing that they are hopelessly in love with each other.

Meanwhile, Don John, an envious and mischief-making malcontent, plots to break the match between Claudio and Hero and employs Conrade and Borachio to assist him. After planting the suspicion in the minds of Claudio and the Prince that Hero is wanton, Don John confirms it by having Borachio talk to Hero's maid, Margaret, at the chamber window at midnight, as if she were Hero. Convinced by this hoax, Claudio and Don Pedro disgrace Hero before the altar at the wedding, rejecting her as unchaste. Shocked by the allegation, which her father readily accepts, Hero swoons away and the priest, who believes in her innocence, intervenes. At his suggestion, she is secretly sent to her uncle's home and publicly reported dead in order to soften the hearts of her accusers as well as lessen the impact of gossip. Leonato is grief–stricken.

Benedick and Beatrice, their sharp wit blunted by the pain of the slander, honestly confess their love for each other before the same altar. Benedick proves his love by challenging his friend, Claudio, to a duel to requite the honor of Beatrice's cousin, Hero. Borachio, overheard by the watch as he boasts of his false meeting with Hero to Conrade, is taken into the custody of Constable Dogberry and clears Hero; but Don John has fled. Her innocence confirmed, her father, satisfied with Claudio's penitent demeanor, directs him to hang verses on her tomb that night and marry his niece, sight unseen, the next morning, which Claudio agrees to do, in a double wedding with Beatrice and Benedick. He joyfully discovers that the masked lady he has promised to marry is Hero. The play ends with an account of Don John being detained by the local authorities.

Estimated Reading Time

Much Ado About Nothing was written to be performed before an audience, without intermission, in less than three hours. Allow your imagination full sway in a straight–through, first reading to grasp the plot and characters. This should take about three hours. To understand the play's nuances, reread it and take note of the usage of each word glossed at the bottom of the text. This should take about one hour per act. Observe how the syntax assigned to each character reveals their pattern of thought. Give yourself enough time to explore the play. While you enjoy the humor, language, and the composition, chuckle along with Shakespeare, at our human vanities.

You can use audiotapes, available at libraries, to follow the text and hear the changing rhythms of verse and prose that this play is famous for. Videotaped performances are also available. Study groups may easily read the piece aloud.

SECTION TWO

Act I

Act I, Scene I (pages 1–8)

New Characters:

Leonato: *governor of Messina and father of Hero, a man of manners and hospitality, whose conventionality will be tested by the depth of his grief*

Hero: *Leonato's only child, a docile and conventional young woman, honored for her chastity*

Beatrice: *Leonato's spirited niece, gifted with a brilliant wit and interested in Benedick*

Messenger: *brings news of Prince Don Pedro's victory and approach to Messina*

Don Pedro: *prince of Aragon, who victoriously returns from battle against his illegitimate brother for his throne; Leonato's guest during his stay in Messina and enjoys matchmaking*

Claudio: *young count, Don Pedro's courageous right–hand man, who seeks the hand of Hero; a man who relies on his outer senses, will be duped by Don John into shaming Hero*

Benedick: *quick–witted and spirited young count who, though an avowed misogynist, is attracted to Beatrice*

Balthasar: *musician, an attendant on Don Pedro*

Don John: *Don Pedro's malcontented, illegitimate brother who resents Don Pedro and Claudio and will do anything to cross them*

Summary

The scene takes place before Leonato's house. The messenger informs Leonato that victorious Don Pedro, Prince of Aragon, will arrive shortly with his favorite, Lord Claudio of Florence, who performed courageously in battle. Beatrice asks about Lord Benedick of Padua and learns that he has returned a hero. Don Pedro arrives with his valiant lords, Claudio and Benedick, his attendant, Balthasar, and his bastard brother, Don John. Leonato and Don Pedro exchange niceties and Beatrice outspars Benedick in a spirited word–match during which Benedick calls Beatrice "disdainful" and Beatrice calls Benedick a "pernicious suitor." Leonato invites Don Pedro, Claudio, and Benedick to be his guests during their visit. All exit but Benedick and Claudio.

Claudio confesses his attraction to Hero and his desire to marry her if she be modest. Benedick reveals his attraction to Beatrice, "were she not possessed with a fury," and wonders if there is any man who does not fear his wife will be unfaithful. Don Pedro returns and, hearing of Claudio's love for Hero, attests to her chastity and offers to arrange the marriage, by first wooing Hero (disguised as Claudio), then asking Leonato for her hand. And, Benedick professes both his misogyny and his unwillingness to marry.

Analysis

The exposition advises us that all the players are acquainted. Hero immediately recognizes Beatrice's oblique reference to Benedick as "Signor Mountanto," Leonato refers to the long–standing "merry war betwixt Signor Benedick" and Beatrice, and Claudio confesses his attraction to Hero before leaving for the war. This level of intimacy introduces a mimetic realism, much like that in *Hamlet*—giving credibility to the character's actions and easing their confrontations—that is sustained throughout the play. Approximately 75 percent of the play is written in prose, a style nearer to colloquial speech than verse. Both the prose and the verse sound with the vitality of Shakespeare's musical style.

The mask motif, predominant in this play, is emphasized by Benedick and Beatrice and subtly disguised as clever diatribe in the roles that they assume to hide their obsession with each other. Fashion imagery, a symbol of appearance versus reality, is introduced as Beatrice states that Benedick "wears his faith but as the fashion of his hat" and Benedick calls "courtesy a turncoat." Their wordspar reveals they are memory–locked, but Shakespeare indicates that their relationship will take a turn for the better by the choice of their names—Benedictus means blessed and Beatrice means blesser.

Beatrice's inquiry about Benedick, though well–seasoned with sarcasm, shows her concern about his welfare as she elicits information about whether he returned safely, if he performed well in battle, and the identity of his present associates. Hero's single line in this scene indicates her modest and retiring nature, builds suspense about her character, and subdues interest in her as emphasis is put on Beatrice, who observes everything around her with a relentlessly playful and unrestrained wit. Benedick momentarily lifts his mask to reveal that his misogyny is assumed as a whetstone for his wit, but closes it quickly.

Claudio suspiciously asks Don Pedro if he praises Hero merely "to fetch [him] in" and Don Pedro protests, both lines serving to initiate a symmetrical pattern which Benedick completes with greater force, stridently using musical imagery in his verbal assaults upon the holy state of marriage, creating an ensemble structure with Claudio and Don Pedro playing his willing straight men.

Since marrying an heiress was a young man's best opportunity, Claudio's first question to Don Pedro is, "Hath Leonato any son, my lord?" Don Pedro's plan, to disguise himself as Claudio in order to win Hero for him at the masked ball, renews the mask motif as a well–intentioned deception. This motif sets the stage for the plot, which turns on a series of misunderstandings and deceptions: a quest for honesty and mutual respect as each character learns to discriminate properly and to estimate everything at its true value. This scene is written in prose up to the bottom of page 7, then continues in verse.

Study Questions

1. Who was victorious in the battle that preceded the opening of the play?

2. What is the relationship between Don Pedro, Claudio, and Benedick?

3. Why is the speech of Leonato, Don Pedro, and Claudio so rigid? What does their style tell us about their characters?

4. How does Beatrice cover up her concern for Benedick?

5. What simile does Beatrice use to describe Benedick's faith?

6. During their wordspar, what accusations do Benedick and Beatrice hurl on each other?

7. What is the greatest fear of Claudio and Benedick?

8. Have the characters met before?

9. What about Hero is of major concern to Claudio?

10. Which character reveals his misogyny? Is this misogyny real?

Answers

1. Prince Don Pedro of Aragon won the battle.

2. Both Claudio and Benedick fought bravely for the prince.

3. The speech of Leonato, Don Pedro, and Claudio shows their adherence to courtly manners and rituals. Their style betrays an addiction to convention.

4. Beatrice covers her concern for Benedick through her witty downgrading of him.

5. Beatrice states that Benedick wears his faith but as the fashion of his hat.

6. Benedict accuses Beatrice of being disdainful and Beatrice accuses Benedict of being a pernicious lover.

7. Both Claudio and Benedick fear becoming cuckolds.

8. Yes, they have met before.

9. Claudio is concerned about Hero's chastity.

10. Benedick reveals his misogyny. The misogyny is merely a whetstone for his wit.

Suggested Essay Topics

1. Contrast the forms of language used by Leonato, Don Pedro, and Claudio with that of Benedick and Beatrice. Why did Shakespeare give them differing forms of expression? What do these forms tell you about the nature of the characters and the probable direction the play will take? Who are the least predictable and most predictable characters and why?

2. Shakespeare has introduced the concept of masks, or deception, at the onset of the play. Cite the use of this concept. What information does this give us about the theme of the play?

3. Beatrice masks her concern for Benedick with her wit. What does the dialogue suggest about their prior encounters and future encounters? Use the text to explain.

4. When Claudio asks Benedick about Hero's modesty, Benedick responds by asking whether Claudio wants an honest response or his customary macho response. What does this tell you about Benedick's awareness of his own nature? Using the text, discuss Benedick's answer to Claudio's question.

Act I, Scene II (page 9)

New Character:

Antonio: *Leonato's brother*

Summary

In Leonato's house, Antonio advises his brother that his servant overheard the prince, Don Pedro, tell Claudio that he loved Hero and that he would reveal this to her at the dance to be held at Leonato's house that night. And, if she found him suitable, he would request her hand from Leonato. Leonato asks Antonio to convey this information to Hero, so she can also prepare her answer should the report he has just heard be true.

Analysis

Noting (which can mean observing, overhearing, and musical notation) is an obvious pun in the title (Elizabethans pronounced nothing/noting alike) and is central to the major theme of this play: appearance versus reality. This theme is continued by having the conversation between Claudio and Don Pedro overheard by a servant, who repeats it to his master, Antonio, who repeats it to his brother, Leonato, who advises him to repeat it to his daughter, Hero, so she, a commoner, can prepare her response to the prince. This brief scene, written in prose, advises us of the speed with which news travels in Messina and complicates the plot with misinformation based on the servant's partial eavesdropping. Hearsay leads to a number of partings between the characters in this play. The word *ado* in the title may also be a pun on the French word for farewell, *adieu*, so common in usage that we find it in the dialogue of the play. Note that musicians enter to work for Leonato (26).

Study Questions

1. Who overheard the conversation between Claudio and Don Pedro, and where did he hear it?

2. Why does Antonio tell his brother about this conversation?

3. What is the misinformation conveyed in this scene?

4. How quickly does news travel in Messina and in what manner?

5. How did this misinformation probably come about?

6. How is "nothing" used as a pun in the title of this play?

7. Is there any other word used in the title of the play which might also be a pun?

8. What does the action of the scene tell us about hearsay?

9. Leonato prefers to treat the information he received in this scene as a dream. Why?

10. Who will tell Hero the news?

Answers

1. Antonio's servant overheard the information in the orchard.

2. Antonio tells Leonato about this conversation in order to prepare him for the situation and give him some time to prepare his answer.

3. The misinformation conveyed in this scene is that the prince is in love with Hero and will ask her hand in marriage for himself.

4. News travels very quickly in Messina and is spread by word-of-mouth.

5. The misinformation of the servant is most likely due to the fact that he heard only part of Don Pedro's and Claudio's conversation.

6. Nothing was pronounced like noting during Elizabethan times.

7. "Ado" may be a pun for *adieu*, the French word for farewell, which characterizes the characters' formal breakups as a result of the misinformation generated in the play.

8. The action of this scene tells us that hearsay is oft repeated.

9. Leonato treats the information he learned in this scene as a dream because it is hard for him to readily accept the reality that the prince is in love with and wants to marry his daughter, a commoner.

10. Leonato directed Antonio, her uncle, to tell Hero of the prince's plans.

Suggested Essay Topics

1. In the text, Leonato refuses Antonio's offer to send for the eavesdropping servant. Why? Does he not wish to enlarge on the report? Does he not wish to seem over–anxious? Does he trust his brother implicitly? Explain.

2. In a town where news travels quickly, who else might the servant tell his report to? Might the town now have two rumored suitors for Hero's hand? What kinds of gossip

would this lead to? Compare the way news travels in Messina to the ways in which news travels in your community. Are they similar or different?

Act I, Scene III (pages 10–11)

New Characters:

Conrade: *Don John's companion, who assumes the position of advisor*

Borachio: *Don John's companion, recently employed by Leonato, who will play a major role in the slander of Hero*

Summary

We are still at Leonato's house. Conrade greets Don John, only to find him in a foul mood. When he attempts to reason Don John out of his misery, Don John takes a perverse and self-willed stance. Conrade advises Don John that he needs to bide his time, reminding him that he is too recently taken back in Don Pedro's good graces, after having confronted him in battle, before resuming his mischief. Don John insists on following his own course, stating that his plain–dealing villainy is more virtuous than flattery and reveals his bitterness at any expectation of humility on his part. As Conrade suggests that he make use of his discontent, Borachio enters to inform Don John that his brother is being entertained by Leonato and that, while employed at Leonato's, he overheard the prince tell Claudio that he will woo Hero for himself, then give her to him. Envious of Claudio's standing as the prince's right-hand man, Don John engages Conrade and Borachio to help him to destroy the count, and goes to the party.

Analysis

The counterplot to the Hero-Claudio plot is introduced through the mean-spirited character of Don John, illegitimate heir to Prince Don Pedro's throne, revealed with pounding alliterative phrases, "moral medicine" and "mortifying mischief," who, although accepted back into the prince's good graces after challenging his throne, is incapable of any gratitude and marinates in his one–dimensional misery. His hanger-ons, Conrade and Borachio, are willing to assist him in any mischief in order to be in his good graces. Don John's casual use of astrological language in his allusion to Conrade being born under the planet Saturn, a signature of cold ambition and sullenness, indicates its common usage in Shakespeare's time.

We learn that news of the marriage is still being overheard and travelling quickly, and Don John intends to take advantage of it to ruin his adversaries. In contrast to the preceding scenes, the only allusion to music here is Don John's out-of-tune statement that he has decreed "not to sing in my cage." This prose scene shows traces of verse.

Study Questions

1. How is Don John related to Don Pedro?

2. What is Don John's mood in this scene?

3. Under what planet is Conrade born?

4. What kind of advice does Conrade give Don John?

5. How does Don John respond to Conrade's advice?

6. What information does Borachio bring to Don John?

7. What effect does this information have on Don John?

8. Why are Conrade and Borachio willing to assist Don John?

9. Where does Don John go at the end of the scene?

10. How does Shakespeare use repetition and contrast in this scene?

Answers

1. Don John is Don Pedro's illegitimate brother.

2. Don John's mood is foul, based on his willfulness and impatience.

3. Conrade is born under the planet Saturn.

4. Conrade, hoping to appeal to Don John's ambitions, advises

        him to stay within the prince's good graces until he is able
        to devise a solid plan to undo his brother and his court.

5. Don John tells Conrade he has no intention of following
     anyone's will, even for the sake of flattery, other than his
     own.

6. Borachio informs Don John that the prince is being enter-
     tained at supper at Leonato's, where he will woo Hero for
     Claudio.

7. Don John, envious of Claudio because he bested him in
     battle, decides to cross him.

8. Conrade and Borachio agree to help Don John in his decep-
     tion in order to satisfy their own ambitions, should Don
     John one day become prince.

9. Don John goes to Leonato's house to join the party given
     for his brother Don Pedro, and to seek a means of crossing
     Claudio.

10. In this scene, Shakespeare repeats the motif of noting, or
     eavesdropping, with Borachio, and contrasts Don John's
     resentment with Don Pedro's forgiveness. Stylistically, Don
     John's clipped, obsessive speech is void of any geniality.

Suggested Essay Topics

1. Today, unlike the time about which Shakespeare writes,
     illegitimacy is accepted. Do you think that Don John has a
     right to resent the world for being born a bastard? Can you
     think of any argument that would bring about a change of
     mind in him? Why do you think Conrade advises him to be
     patient and to practice flattery?

2. Borachio is revealed as an informer who will aid Don John.
     What kind of a man do you think he is? Ironically, he acci-
     dentally obtained his information while employed as a
     perfumer at Leonato's house. Why do you suppose this is
     the method Shakespeare used to convey this information
     to Don John? How is the word odor used in terms of reputa-
     tion? Explain.

SECTION THREE

Act II

Act II, Scene I (pages 13–22)

New Characters:

Margaret and Ursula: *waiting gentlewomen to Hero*

Summary

While Leonato's household awaits the arrival of the maskers, Beatrice tells us that no man is her match and she advises Hero on how to answer the prince when he seeks her hand. The maskers arrive and we are treated to a variety of deceits as they dance. Don Pedro, pretending to be Claudio, takes Hero aside. Beatrice, pretending that she does not know that she is speaking with Benedick, uses the opportunity to call him a fool. All exit except Don John, Borachio, and Claudio.

Don John and Borachio purposefully mistake Claudio for Benedick and tell him that Don Pedro is in love with Hero and swore he would marry her that night. Claudio, believing their deception, is joined by Benedick who teases him about losing Hero. Claudio leaves and Benedick reflects on his conversation with Beatrice.

Don Pedro, Hero, and Leonato return. Don Pedro assures Benedick that his wooing was on Claudio's behalf. When Claudio and Beatrice return, Benedick exits to avoid Beatrice. Don Pedro announces that he has won Hero for Claudio, and Leonato concurs. When Beatrice leaves, Don Pedro observes that Beatrice would be an excellent wife for Benedick, and enlists Leonato, Claudio, and Hero to aid him in making a match.

Analysis

The masquerade ball, fashionable in Tudor England, and the guessing game it engenders, emphasizes the problem of knowing/not knowing, which leads to harmony/disharmony. In this scene, Shakespeare offers us both actual music and musical metaphor (Don Pedro teaching birds to sing, i.e., to love).

Claudio's inclination to jealousy and his reliance upon sense information not only leads him to believe Don John's deceit but foreshadows the tragic action he will take at his nuptials. Hero, too proper to do anything but acquiesce in her father's choice, reveals nothing about her feelings for Claudio. Benedick, stung by Beatrice's description of him as little more than a court jester, wonders how she can know him and not know him, ignoring the fact that he said her wit was out of the *Hundred Merry Tales*, a coarse book. The infection of this sting swells toward the end of the scene—when he requests that Don Pedro send him on any absurd mission rather than have three words with Beatrice—and will not be lanced until the end of the act. Beatrice reveals her previous relationship with Benedick when she speaks of his heart (265–68):

> Indeed, my lord, he lent it me awhile; and I gave him
> use for it, a double heart for his single one:
> marry, once before he won it of me with false dice,
> therefore your Grace may well say I have lost it.

Only Don Pedro, dazzled by her lively sallies with him on the topic of marriage, exhibits a flash of intuitive knowledge as he moves past the outer appearance given by Beatrice's mock logic and clever comedy to see her as "an excellent wife for Benedick."

This scene begins and ends with emphasis on Beatrice's unwillingness to consider marriage, which parallels Benedick's diatribe on marriage and sets the tone for the double gulling scenes to come; the counterplot to Beatrice and Benedick's seeming disaffection for each other.

Fashion imagery is continued in this scene. Benedick describes Beatrice as "the infernal Ate" (Greek goddess personifying foolhardy and ruinous impulse) "in good apparel," and Beatrice tells Don Pedro, "[y]our Grace is too costly to wear every day." Note the appearance of rhymed fourteeners (87–8) and Claudio's speech of 11 lines of end–stopped verse (159–69).

Study Questions

1. To what dances does Beatrice compare wooing, wedding and repenting?

2. Whom does Ursula dance with and how does she recognize him?

3. What statement of Benedick's preceded Beatrice's put–down of him during the dance?

4. Whom does Don John purposefully mistake for Benedick?

5. Which characters have soliloquies in this act?

6. Would Benedick marry Beatrice if she were "endowed with all that Adam had left him before he transgressed"?

7. Was Don Pedro able to win Hero for Claudio?

8. When will Claudio and Hero's wedding take place?

9. Whom does Don Pedro think would be an excellent wife for Benedick?

10. Leonato predicts that Benedick and Beatrice, after one week of marriage, will be in what condition?

Answers

1. Beatrice compares wooing to a Scotch jig, wedding to a measure, and repenting to a cinquepace.

2. Ursula is dancing with Antonio, Leonato's brother. She recognizes him by the waggling of his head and the dryness of his hand.

3. Benedick told Beatrice that someone had told him that she was disdainful and had her wit out of the *Hundred Merry Tales*.

4. Don John purposefully mistakes Claudio for Benedick.

5. Claudio and Benedick have soliloquies in this act.

6. No, Benedick would not marry Beatrice, even if she were

endowed with all that Adam had left him before he transgressed.

7. Yes, Don Pedro was able to win Hero for Claudio.

8. Claudio and Hero will marry seven days later, on a Monday.

9. Don Pedro thinks that Beatrice would be an excellent wife
for Benedick.

10. Leonato predicts that Benedick and Beatrice would, if married but one week, talk themselves mad.

Suggested Essay Topics

1. Why is Claudio so easily deceived by Don John and Borachio? How does he respond to the deception? What does his
soliloquy tell you about his character?

2. Using the text, explain what happened off stage during
Benedick's dance with Beatrice? How do we know this happened? What effect did this have on Beatrice?

3. What effect did his dance with Beatrice have on Benedick?
Does Beatrice know him and not know him? Is there any
truth in her statement that he is Don John's court jester?
How does he respond to Beatrice afterward? How do you
think he'll respond to her in the future? Explain, citing lines
from the text.

4. Don Pedro considers Beatrice a good match for Benedick,
while Leonato thinks they'll talk themselves to death in a
week. Who do you agree with? Why? Use the text to defend
your position.

Act II, Scene II (pages 22–23)

Summary

Borachio tells Don John that he can cross the marriage of
Claudio and Hero. Don John jumps at the opportunity. Borachio
lays out his plan to have Margaret, Hero's waiting–gentlewoman,
look out her mistress' window the night before the wedding and

be mistaken for Hero, while he, Borachio, woos her. He directs Don John to tell Don Pedro that he has dishonored himself by arranging a marriage between Claudio and a common trollop, and then offer him proof of Hero's disloyalty by bringing him to witness the staged deceit. Don John accepts the plan and offers Borachio a fee of a thousand ducats.

Analysis

Borachio, recently employed as a perfumer at Leonato's, is the directive force of this prose scene. Don John, disappointed that his ploy to break the friendship between Don Pedro and Claudio failed, willingly accepts Borachio's plan and direction to destroy the planned marriage of Claudio and Hero, which moves the counterplot forward and prepares the audience for the crisis to come.

The plan hinges on Don John's ability to persuade Don Pedro that he has dishonored himself, and the coldness of Don John assures us that he will have no second thoughts about implementing this action. His offer of a large fee to Borachio ensures that Borachio will play his part well. Shakespeare emphasizes the sourness of this scene's note by placing it between two musical scenes. At this point the first movement of action, dominated by Don Pedro, in the role of matchmaker, ends and we look forward to seeing the marriage–mockers reformed and the villain defeated.

Study Questions

1. What is the first thing that Borachio tells Don John?
2. Who is the architect of the plan to slander Hero?
3. What does Don John state would be medicinable to him?
4. What did Borachio tell Don John a year ago?
5. What role has been assigned to Don John in this plan?
6. Who will be mistaken for Hero?
7. What role will Borachio play?
8. What effect do the plotters expect to have on the prince, Claudio, Hero, and Leonato?

9.   How is the only way the plan will succeed?

10. How much will Don John pay Borachio for his deceit?

Answers

1.   The first thing Borachio tells Don John is that he can cross the marriage between Claudio and Hero.

2.   Borachio is the architect of the plan to slander Hero.

3.   Don John states that any cross, any impediment to the marriage of Claudio would be medicinable to him.

4.   Borachio told Don John that he is in the favor of Margaret, Hero's waiting-gentlewoman.

5.   Don John's role is to first plant the slander in Don Pedro's mind and then to offer him proof.

6.   Margaret will be mistaken for Hero.

7.   Borachio will play the role of Hero's lover.

8.   The plotters intend to misuse the prince, to vex Claudio, to undo Hero, and to kill Leonato.

9.   The plan will only succeed if Don John can first convince Don Pedro that his honor has been sullied by arranging the alliance between Claudio and Hero.

10. Don John will pay Borachio a thousand ducats for his deceit.

Suggested Essay Topics

1.   Who designed and is directing the slander against Hero? What is the plan? How will it be brought about? What roles have been assigned and to whom? Cite the text to explain.

2.   Do you think Borachio's plan will succeed? What do you think the responses of Don Pedro and Claudio are likely to be? Would you fall for such a hoax? Explain.

3.   What are the motives of the plotters? Are they the same or different? Can any motive ever justify slander? What values does a slanderer lack? Explain.

Act II, Scene III (pages 24–30)

New Character:

Boy: *sent by Benedick to fetch a book*

Summary

The scene takes place in Leonato's garden. Benedick reflects on love and marriage. He hides himself in the arbor when Don Pedro, Leonato, and Claudio enter. Pretending not to note his presence, they listen as Balthasar sings a song about the deceptions of men. Then they speak of Beatrice's love for Benedick, which they claim they learned from Hero. Benedick does not believe it to be a gull because Leonato is involved. They detail the depth of Beatrice's passion and frustration, fearful that she will harm herself because of it, then list her virtues. They agree that Benedick is too scornful to be told of the matter and exit. Reflecting on what he has just heard, Benedick acknowledges to himself his love for Beatrice. Beatrice, sent by Don Pedro to call Benedick to dinner, is perceived by Benedick in a new light as he looks for evidence of her affection for him.

Analysis

The second movement of action, which propels this play into high comedy, begins now and continues through the first scene of Act IV. Highly theatrical, this is Benedick's chief scene in the play, the one his lines have been building toward and the one on which the validity of the rest of his actions depend. The phrasing of the soliloquies, well–written for stage delivery and the actor's memory, require a balanced performance with inventive stage business (player's actions that establish atmosphere, reveal character, or explain a situation) to succeed. The scene takes place in the evening, before supper. It is written in prose except for 21 lines of blank verse spoken by Don Pedro and Claudio (page 25). The new character, the boy, perhaps serves as an image of innocence, or possibly the line was written for the child of one of the company members to play.

Ironically, in Benedick's pre–gulling soliloquy, amply full
of his usual self–satisfied, machismo rhetoric, he wonders, for
a moment, if he may be so converted as to see with the same
eyes of love he has just expressed contempt for. In this moment,
Benedick's character initiates a new level of awareness by step-
ping out from his position as clever onlooker and seeing himself
as part of the comedy of human behavior. Although he immediately dismisses the thought, he proceeds to share his ideal woman
with us (page 24):

> One woman is fair, yet I am well; another is wise,
> yet I am well; another virtuous, yet I am well:
> but till all graces be in one woman, one woman
> shall not come in my grace. Rich she shall be,
> that's certain; wise; or I'll none; mild, or come
> not near me; noble, or not I for an angel; of good
> discourse, an excellent musician; and her hair
> shall be of what colour it please God.

Shakespeare references and thereby emphasizes the title of
this play with a musical extension of the pun on "noting" and
"nothing" before Balthasar sings a love song, which serves to
soften Benedick, although he dismisses Balthasar's singing as
a dog's howl. As the gullers proceed to speak of Beatrice's love
for him, Benedick's comments about them abate, and he eaves-
drops in blank amazement. They cite in her the very virtues
he demanded before their arrival. The irony is that Don Pedro,
Claudio, and Leonato think they are lying about Beatrice's love for
Benedick, when, in fact, they are telling the truth.

In his post–gulling soliloquy, a chastened Benedick steps forward and speaks directly for the first time (page 29):

> This can be no trick: the conference was sadly
> borne. They have the truth of this from Hero. They
> seem to pity the lady: it seems her affections have
> their full bent. Love me! Why, it must be requited. I
> hear how I am censured: they say I will bear myself
> proudly, if I perceive the love come from her; they
> say too that she will rather die than give any sign

of affection. I did never think to marry: I must
not seem proud: happy are they that hear their
detractions, and can put them to mending.

The passage reveals that Benedick has undergone an attitude adjustment from which he emerges with an expanded conscience, a humbled ego, and an intuitive understanding of his real feelings for Beatrice, then he bursts into his old effusiveness with the declaration that he will love Beatrice "most horribly" and climaxes with the comedic hyperbole, "the world must be peopled." At this point, Shakespeare sends in Beatrice, which heightens the comedic value of the scene as Benedick, a confirmed bachelor turned love fanatic, spies "some marks of love" in her curt speeches. This is a prose scene except for 21 lines of blank verse.

Study Questions

1. What is orthography? Who has turned orthography?
2. What graces does Benedick seek in a woman?
3. To what does Benedick liken Balthasar's singing?
4. When does Shakespeare reference the title of the play?
5. Why does Benedick dismiss the thought that he is being gulled?
6. From whom do the plotters claim to have received their information?
7. Who fears that Beatrice will die and why?
8. How in love with Beatrice does Benedick declare he will be?
9. Did Beatrice call Benedick into dinner on her own initiative?
10. At the end of the scene, what does Benedick spy in Beatrice?

Answers

1. Webster defines orthography as the art of writing words with the proper letters according to standard usage. Claudio has turned orthography.

2. Benedick expects a woman to be rich, wise, virtuous, mild, noble, of good discourse, and an excellent musician.

3. Benedick likens Balthasar's singing to a dog howling.

4. Shakespeare references the title of the play before gulling Benedick.

5. Benedick dismisses the thought that he is being gulled because he does not believe that an elder such as Leonato would be in on such a plot.

6. The plotters claim to have received their information from Hero.

7. Hero fears that Beatrice will die because of her unrequited love for Benedick.

8. Benedick declares that he will be horribly in love with Beatrice.

9. No, she did not. Against her will, Beatrice was sent to call Benedick into dinner.

10. Benedick spies some marks of love in Beatrice at the end of this scene.

Suggested Essay Topics

1. Why do you think Shakespeare chooses the moment of Benedick's gulling to remind us of the title of the play? Why does he use flattery to ensnare Benedick? Is Benedick actually misled by the gull or does the gull offer him the opportunity to own a part of himself he had denied? Explain.

2. Compare Benedick's two soliloquies. Do they reveal a change in consciousness? Describe the change in consciousness, citing the text.

3. How are Benedick's speeches, before and after the gulling, handled stylistically? Do they have theatrical value? Explain, citing specific passages from the play. How do you imagine an actor would play this role? Describe specific stage business the actor would employ.

Act III

Act III, Scene I (pages 31–34)

Summary

The scene takes place in the garden. Hero sets the trap for Beatrice by sending Margaret to tell Beatrice that she is the subject of Hero and Ursula's gossip. Beatrice appears instantly and follows them, hidden among the honeysuckle, to eavesdrop. Hero and Ursula speak of Benedick's unrequited love for Beatrice and Beatrice's disdainful scorn for Benedick. They speak of Benedick's virtues and Beatrice's faults, concluding that Beatrice is too self–endeared to be told of the matter. Hero, feigning exasperation, tells Ursula that she will devise some honest slander to poison Benedick's love for Beatrice and thereby save him from wasting away with love. Alone, reflecting on what she has just heard, Beatrice surrenders contempt and maiden pride, determined to accept Benedick's love.

Analysis

A day has passed since the gulling of Benedick. This charming parallel scene is written wholly in verse, most of which is end–stopped, and terminates with a 10-line stanza composed of quatrains and a couplet. We find the usually loquacious Beatrice quietly listening, and you can be sure that any skilled actress will find a variety of attitudes to express in this silence. Surprisingly, quiet and docile Hero mischievously leads the gull. Beatrice's soliloquy shows her lyric response to their conversation (107–16); it is short and to the point:

> What fire is in mine ears? Can this be true?
> Stand I condemn'd for pride and scorn so much?
> Contempt, farewell! and maiden pride, adieu!
> No glory lives behind the back of such.
> And, Benedick, love on; I will requite thee,
> Taming my wild heart to thy loving hand.
> If thou dost love, my kindness shall incite thee
> To bind our loves up in a holy band;
> For others say thou dost deserve, and I
> Believe it better than reportingly.

Through a series of parallels, Shakespeare has brought both Benedick and Beatrice from feigned antipathy to mutual romantic idealism. Beatrice's simple, humble, intuitive acceptance of her faults and her willingness to change foreshadows the intimacy of her next meeting with Benedick.

The scene is short but believable. There is no reason to extend this scene because we know from the first scene of the play that Beatrice's concern for Benedick is real, though guarded due to an earlier perceived rejection by him. Since we've witnessed Benedick's change, we readily accept her change.

Study Questions

1. On whom do Hero and Ursula play the gull?

2. Where is Beatrice during this scene?

3. Who told Hero that Benedick was in love with Beatrice?

4. What character defects does Hero ascribe to Beatrice?

5. How would Beatrice treat a fair-faced man?

6. Why does Hero say it is useless to mention these defects of character to Beatrice?

7. What counsel does Hero intend to give to Benedick?

8. Which scene in the play does this one parallel?

9. How does Cupid kill?

10. Which faults does Beatrice willingly give up in her soliloquy?

Answers

1. Hero and Ursula play the gull on Beatrice.

2. Beatrice is hidden in the honeysuckle arbor.

3. Don Pedro and Claudio told Hero that Benedick was in love with Beatrice.

4. Hero states that Beatrice is disdainful, scornful, and full of intellectual pride.

5. Beatrice would swear that the gentleman be her sister.

6. Hero says that it is useless to mention these defects of character to Beatrice because Beatrice would respond with mockery.

7. Hero intends to counsel Benedick to fight against his passions.

8. This scene parallels the preceding scene, in which Benedick was similarly gulled.

9. Cupid kills some with arrows, some with traps.

10. Beatrice willingly surrenders contempt and maiden pride in her soliloquy.

Suggested Essay Topics

1. Why does Beatrice accept the gull so willingly? Why is she able to surrender her faults so freely? What does this tell you about the true nature of her character? Explain.

2. What does Beatrice mean when she says that "others say thou [Benedick] doest deserve, and I believe it better than reportingly"? What is a better evidence than mere report? Where is it found? Why is this evidence more reliable for Beatrice? Explain.

3. If you were directing this play, how would you manage this scene? What stage business would you give to Beatrice, Hero, and Ursula? What would be the overall tone? Explain fully.

Act III, Scene II (pages 34–37)

Summary

It is the night before the wedding. Don Pedro announces he will depart for Aragon right after the nuptials. He refuses Claudio's offer to accompany him. Don Pedro and Claudio observe a change in Benedick, including a shaved face and pristine habits of personal hygiene, and tease him about it. Benedick, unusually sober in demeanor, protests that he has a toothache. He invites Leonato to walk with him in order to enter into a short but private conversation. Don John enters. He tells Don Pedro and Claudio that Hero is disloyal and invites them to go with him to witness her chamber window entered that night at midnight. Claudio vows to shame Hero before the congregation if he witnesses such disloyalty that evening and Don Pedro vows to join him in disgracing Hero.

Analysis

Although this prose scene opens in a relaxed manner, the pacing of the play is speeding up to propel us toward the crisis in Act IV. Claudio's prompt offer to leave with the prince, rather than stay for his honeymoon, indicates that he loves Hero as an image to be possessed rather than as a person to be explored. This does not surprise us since he kept his interest in her on the back burner until the war was over. We see a new and reflective Benedick, unwilling to play court jester and no longer completing Claudio and Don John's lines with witty rejoinders, hidden behind the excuse of a toothache. His memorable line from this scene is "everyone can master a grief but he that has it." Don Pedro and Claudio use clothes imagery to tease clean–shaven, perfumed, and fashionably dressed Benedick, who takes Leonato offstage for a few short words, presumably about Beatrice, to avoid his friends' jesting. At this point the two harmoniously interwoven major plots begin a polarization, not to be reconciled until the solution, forming a strong dramatic rhythm.

The confusions thrown on the path of the action of the play have prepared us for this moment and the major action of this scene arrives with Don John and unfolds as he puts the scheme to slander Hero into action. Characterized as an observer rather than a participator, he knows exactly how to trap his prey, appealing to Don Pedro's reputation and Claudio's jealousy. He dominates the dialogue, feeding Don Pedro and Claudio their lines, which he completes with deceitful sophistry. The subordinate voice pattern Shakespeare assigned to Don Pedro and Claudio, in which their lines had no meaning unless completed by a third party, now traps them tragically (page 37):

Claudio:	May this be so?
Don Pedro:	I will not think it.
Don John:	If you dare not trust that you see, confess not that you know: if you will follow me, I will show you enough; and when you have seen more, and heard more, proceed accordingly.
Claudio:	If I see anything to-night why I should not marry her tomorrow, in the congregation, where I should wed, there will I shame her.
Don Pedro:	And, as I wooed for thee to obtain her, I will join with thee to disgrace her.
Don John:	I will disparage her no farther till you are my witnesses: bear it coldly but till midnight, and let the issue show itself.
Don Pedro:	O day untowardly turned!
Claudio:	O mischief strangely thwarting!
Don John:	O plague right well prevented! So will you say when you have seen the sequel.

Prisoners in Don John's world of sense evidence, they abandon their judgment and adopt his cruel view of the world; Don Pedro and Claudio reflect its emotional scenery as they move into prejudicial and vindictive stances prior to witnessing the evidence. We can easily guess what their response to Don John's hoax will be. The action toward the crisis of the play is now in full spin.

Study Questions

1. When does this scene take place?

2. What is Benedick's observation about grief?

3. Has anyone seen Benedick at the barber's?

4. What does Claudio say about Benedick's jesting spirit?

5. What malady does Benedick claim to have?

6. Who shall be buried with her face upwards?

7. Who invites Leonato to walk aside with him?

8. Why does Don John include Claudio in his conversation?

9. What does Don John tell Don Pedro and Claudio?

10. What invitation does Don John extend to Don Pedro and Claudio?

Answers

1. This scene takes place the night before the wedding.

2. Benedick observes that everyone can master a grief but he that has it.

3. No. But the barber's man has been seen with Benedick.

4. Claudio says that Benedick's jesting spirit is now crept into a lute string and now governed by stops.

5. Benedick claims to suffer from a toothache.

6. Beatrice will be buried with her face upwards.

7. Benedick invites Leonato to walk aside with him.

8. Don John includes Claudio in his conversation because the matter he speaks of concerns him.

9. Don John tells Don Pedro and Claudio that Hero is disloyal.

10. Don John invites Don Pedro and Claudio to witness Hero's disloyalty with their own eyes and ears.

Suggested Essay Topics

1. What does the change in Benedick's dialogue and demeanor tell us about Benedick? Why will he no longer play the fool? What few words does he wish to have with Leonato? What

does this indicate about the stance his character will take in the future?

2. Why was Don John so easily able to plant suspicion about the chastity of Hero in the minds of Don Pedro and Claudio? What does this tell us about their characters? What do you imagine will be their reaction when they see the staged deceit? Describe the probable scene.

3. Stylistically, what syntactic pattern does Shakespeare use to trap Don Pedro and Claudio in Don John's deceit? What does this pattern tell you about the character's thinking habits? Why was it effective? Explain.

Act III, Scene III (pages 38–42)

New Characters:

Dogberry: *illiterate master constable, whose love of high-faluting words is only matched by his misuse of them, he exposes the slanderous deception, thereby saving Hero*

Verges: *headborough, or parish constable, Dogberry's elderly companion*

First Watchman and Second Watchman: *Dogberry's assistants, who providentially overhear Borachio describe the details of the deception perpetrated upon Hero*

Summary

The scene takes place at night, on the street, to the side of the door of Leonato's house. Master Constable Dogberry, bearing a lantern, and his elder compartner, Verges, arrive with the watch. Dogberry gives them their charge, specifically instructing them to watch about Leonato's door because of the preparations for the marriage. Borachio staggers forth from Leonato's, followed by Conrade, into the drizzling rain. The watch overhear Borachio, his tongue liquor-loose, boast that he earned a thousand ducats for his villainy from Don John. Borachio then discourses upon fashion, calling it a deformed thief. Then he details how he wooed

Margaret, by the name of Hero, while being observed by Don John, Don Pedro, and Claudio from the orchard and how, believing the deceit, Claudio vowed to shame Hero at the wedding before the congregation the next day. The watch immediately takes them into custody.

Analysis

The tragic apprehensions stirred by the last scene are quickly relieved as Shakespeare introduces his broadly comic auxiliary plot in the person of the inimitable Master Constable Dogberry, which brings a common touch to a play peopled with aristocrats. The scene is impeccably timed for the process of discovery and the direction of our dramatic responses and Dogberry's world of language parodies the syntactic landscapes of the other characters in the play and, as he says, "present[s] the prince's own person."

As this prose scene opens, Dogberry instructs the watch with the zaniest misuse of language imaginable—"This is your charge: you shall comprehend all vagrom men," "[y]ou are thought here to be the most senseless and fit man for the constable of the watch," "for the watch to babble and talk is most tolerable and not to be endured," and "be vitigant," all of which translates into normal police procedure—challenge suspicious characters, make no noise, send drunks home, don't strike too quickly and "let [a thief] show himself what he is, and steal out of your company."

Dogberry is the name of a shrub that sprang up in every county of England, a commentary on the constabulatory of Shakespeare's day. The names Otecake and Seacole suggest that the men were dealers in these commodities and trained to read and write. The name Borachio is derived from a Spanish word meaning drunkard.

Seacole follows Dogberry's instructions precisely and directs the watch to stand close as Borachio, "like a true drunkard, utter[s] all," which Shakespeare emphasizes by giving him plenty of sibilants to slur. Borachio brings the clothes imagery, sustained throughout the play, to a climactic point with his seemingly tangential discourse on fashion (pages 40–42):

Borachio:	Thou knowest that the fashions of a doublet, or a hat, or a cloak, is nothing to a man.
Conrade:	Yes, it is apparel.
Borachio:	Tush! I may as well say the fool's the fool. But seest thou not what a deformed thief this fashion is.... Seest thou not, I say, what a deformed thief this fashion is? how giddily a' turns about all the hot bloods between fourteen and five-and-thirty? sometimes fashioning them like Pharaoh's soldiers in the reechy painting, sometime like god Bel's priests in the old church-window, sometime like the shaven Hercules in the smirched worm-eaten tapestry, where his codpiece seems as massy as his club?
Conrade:	All this I see; and I see...that thou hast shifted out of thy tale into telling me of the fashion?
Borachio:	Not so, neither.

He finally gets to the meat of his story. Borachio, architect of this hoax, now repeatedly calls Don John his "master," claiming he made him do it:

	but know that I have to-night wooed Margaret, the Lady Hero's gentlewoman, by the name of Hero: she leans me out at her mistress' chamber-window, bids me a thousand times good night,—I tell this tale vilely:—I should first tell thee how the prince, Claudio and my master, planted and placed and possessed by my master Don John, saw afar off in the orchard this amiable encounter.
Conrade:	And thought they Margaret was Hero?
Borachio:	Two of them did, the prince and Claudio, but the devil my master knew she was Margaret; and partly by his oaths, which first possessed them, partly by the dark night, which did

> deceive them, but chiefly by my villainy, which
> did confirm any slander that Don John had
> made, away went Claudio enraged; swore he
> would meet her, as he was appointed, next
> morning at the temple, and there, before the
> whole congregation, shame her with what
> he saw o'ernight, and send her home again
> without a husband.

At this point, the watch charge him.

Shakespeare surprises us, placing the action of the deceit off–stage. There was no need to slow the action of his play, which, with all its play-acting and deception, has already called attention to its own devices of illusion. Instead, he moves the play forward by embellishing the discovery with a broadly comic brush.

Seacole's recognition of one *Deformed*, is an allusion more popular in Shakespeare's time, but nonetheless funny. One *Deformed* may be a pun on a contemporary's name, possibly French, or a comment on the planet Uranus (in myth, a god maimed by his son, Cronus/Saturn), whose change of signs every seven years introduces an extreme change in fashion and public interest, called the *seven-year-itch* or a person born under that planet. The only thing we know for sure is that he wears a fashionable lock. Borachio's insistence that fashion, i.e., outer semblance, validly relates to his story of deception is a strong clue to the theme of the play.

We now know that Don John's plot will be revealed. Though fools, the watch is effective—they gather evidence before making an accusation, something their betters have not yet learned to do. Shakespeare maintains his comedic stance and prepares us for the scenes to follow by dissolving our tensions into hilarity.

Study Questions

1. Who gives the charge to the watch?

2. How does Dogberry instruct the watch to handle a thief?

3. What is the meaning of the phrase, "my elbow itched"?

4. In what manner does Borachio utter all to Conrade?

5. What does Borachio call a thief?

6. From where did Don John, Don Pedro, and Claudio witness Borachio wooing Margaret in Hero's name?

7. Who believed the staged deceit?

8. What did Claudio swear to do and why?

9. Who charges Borachio and Conrade?

10. How does the watch describe Borachio and Conrade?

Answers

1. Dogberry gives the charge to the watch.

2. Dogberry instructs the watch to, if they take a thief, let him show himself what he is and steal away out of your company.

3. "My elbow itched" is a proverbial warning against questionable companions.

4. Borachio, like a true drunkard, utters all to Conrade.

5. Borachio calls fashion a thief.

6. Don John, Don Pedro, and Claudio were in the orchard when they witnessed Borachio woo Margaret in Hero's name.

7. Don Pedro and Claudio believed the staged deceit.

8. Claudio, enraged, swore to disgrace Hero before the congregation the next morning at their wedding ceremony.

9. Seacole charges Borachio and Conrade.

10. The watch describe Borachio and Conrade as "the most dangerous piece of lechery that ever was known in the commonwealth."

Suggested Essay Topics

1. Explain the comedic value of the watch. How do they move the action of the play forward? Why do you think they are given to such outrageous misuse of language? Despite their lunacy, are they effective? Why?

2. Why did Conrade confess his villainy? Was it only the effect
    of liquor? Was there some other reason? If so, what was it?
    Why do you think so? Explain.

3. Shakespeare has placed the staged deceit off stage. Why? Is
    this effective? Explain.

Act III, Scene IV (pages 42–44)

Summary

The scene is set in the sitting room adjacent to Hero's bed-
chamber. Hero sends Ursula to wake up Beatrice and tell her to
come to the sitting room. Hero and Margaret discuss what she
will wear. Beatrice arrives, sick, and tells Hero it is time to dress
for the wedding. Margaret teasingly suggests to Beatrice that she
take the herb, carduus benedictus, for her malady. Ursula returns
to announce that the wedding party is ready to escort Hero to the
church. The women hasten to the bed-chamber to dress her.

Analysis

This innocent prose scene, on the morning before the wedding, softens us to empathize with Hero. Margaret does not want
Hero to wear a certain rebato, possibly the one she wore in the
staged deceit the night before, but Hero lets us know she has a
mind of her own by insisting on it, dismissing both Margaret and
Beatrice as fools, and Margaret scandalizes Hero with her bawdy
humor. This scene refreshes the fashion imagery and theme of
outer appearance.

Beatrice's illness explains why she slept separately from Hero
the night before; it also affords the ladies the opportunity to
tease her about her new-found love. Margaret, fancying herself
as good a wit as Beatrice, gets in a pointed stab when she advises
Beatrice, "Get you some of this distilled carduus benedictus and
lay it to your heart. It is the only thing for a qualm." And Hero
quips, "There thou prick'st her with a thistle." The pun and double
entendre is obvious. We, with the wedding party, await her as she
runs off to dress.

Study Questions

1. Who does Hero send to wake up Beatrice?

2. What piece of clothing does Margaret try to talk Hero out of wearing?

3. Who does Hero call a fool?

4. Who is not feeling well?

5. Approximately what time is it?

6. What are Beatrice's symptoms?

7. Who attempts to wordspar with Beatrice in this scene?

8. What remedy does Margaret suggest for Beatrice's malady?

9. What is another name for benedictus?

10. What announcement does Ursula bring at the end of the scene?

Answers

1. Hero sends Ursula to wake up Beatrice.

2. Margaret tries to talk Hero out of wearing a specific rebato.

3. Hero calls both Margaret and her cousin, Beatrice, fools.

4. Beatrice is not feeling well.

5. It is approximately five o'clock.

6. Beatrice's symptoms are that she is stuffed and cannot smell.

7. Margaret attempts to wordspar with Beatrice in this scene.

8. Margaret suggests carduus benedictus as a remedy, lain on the heart.

9. Holy thistle is another name for benedictus.

10. Ursula announces that the wedding party has arrived to escort Hero to church.

Suggested Essay Topics

1. Why does Margaret wordspar with Beatrice? Would you say that she is somewhat imitative of Beatrice? How is her style, and her language different from Beatrice? Do you think she could ever win a match with Beatrice? Explain.

2. What is the purpose of this scene? How does it prepare us for the scene that is to follow? What tonal value does it have? Explain.

Act III, Scene V (pages 45–46)

New Character:

Messenger: *calls Leonato to the wedding.*

Summary

The scene takes place in the hall in Leonato's house. Dogberry and Verges visit Leonato just as he is about to leave for the wedding. They chatter, trying Leonato's patience. Finally they tell him that they apprehended two suspicious characters who they want to have examined that morning before him. Leonato instructs them to take the examination and bring it to him. Leonato leaves to give Hero in marriage. Dogberry instructs Verges to send for Francis Seacole, the sexton, to write down the examination which they will take at the jail.

Analysis

Shakespeare provides us with the most suspenseful moment of the play when Dogberry's tediousness and Leonato's impatience collide to prevent the disclosure of Don John's villainy before the wedding. Whatever the matter is, Leonato simply doesn't want to hear it. Ironically, he can't possibly imagine that anything these patronizing and tangential commoners could say would be of any interest to him. The dialogue is painfully funny:

Leonato: Neighbours, you are tedious.

Dogberry: It pleases your worship to say so, but we are the

poor Duke's officers; but truly, for mine own
part, if I were as tedious as a king, I could find
in my heart to bestow it all of your worship.

Leonato: All thy tediousness on me, ah?

Dogberry: Yea, an 'twere a thousand pound more than 'tis;
for I hear as good exclamation on your worship
as of any man in the city; and though I be but a
poor man, I am glad to hear it.

Leonato: I would fain know what you have to say.

Verges then tells him they've taken prisoners, but Dogberry, not
to be upstaged, pursues another loquacious tangent and an exas-
perated Leonato tells Dogberry to examine the prisoners himself.
This is Dogberry's triumph and, fortunately, he will have only the
best, learned writer take his first interrogation and so these men,
"honest as the skin between their brows," who have done their job
and "comprehend[ed] vagrom men," are off to the jail to question
Borachio and Conrade. Knowing that, eventually, the wrong perpetrated against Hero will be righted, we proceed to the wedding.

Study Questions

1. Where does this scene take place?

2. Who visits Leonato in this scene?

3. Why doesn't Leonato listen to them carefully?

4. When Dogberry describes Verges' wits as not so blunt, what
   did he really mean?

5. What is Dogberry's response when Leonato tells him he is
   tedious?

6. What is Leonato's response when he finally understands
   that they have apprehended two people?

7. What hospitality does Leonato offer Dogberry and Verges
   before he leaves?

8. What message is brought to Leonato?

9. What direction does Dogberry give to Verges?

10. Why does Dogberry want a learned writer?

Answers

1. This scene takes place in the hall of Leonato's house.

2. Constable Dogberry and Headborough Verges visit Leonato.

3. Leonato doesn't listen to them carefully because he is distracted with the wedding, and in a hurry to get there.

4. Dogberry meant that Verges' wits were not so sharp.

5. Dogberry, upon being told that he is tedious, returns the compliment.

6. Leonato tells them to take the examination and to bring it to him.

7. Leonato offers wine to Dogberry and Verges.

8. The messenger tells Leonato that the wedding party is waiting for him to give his daughter in marriage.

9. Dogberry directs Verges to go to Francis Seacole and bid him bring his pen and inkhorn to the jail.

10. Dogberry wants a learned writer to set down their excommunication (examination).

Suggested Essay Topics

1. How does this scene serve to move the action of the play forward? How necessary is it to the plot of the play? Would the play make any sense if this scene were cut out by a director? What would have happened to the action of the play if Leonato understood what Dogberry and Verges were talking about? Explain.

2. Why do Dogberry and Verges speak in such a tangential manner? What does their syntax tell you about their thinking processes? Do you think Leonato understood them at all? What did he understand? Cite the passages. If Leonato were not in a hurry to leave, would he have asked them to draw out the exact purpose of their visit? Explain.

Act IV

Act IV, Scene I (pages 47–56)

New Characters:

Friar Francis: *priest at the nuptials of Claudio and Hero, who devises a plan to change the hearts of Claudio and Don Pedro and reverse the effects of the slander*

Attendants: *the bridal party*

Summary

This scene takes place before the altar in the church. Claudio contemptuously rejects Hero as a proved wanton. Leonato assumes that Claudio took Hero's virginity, which Claudio denies. Leonato appeals to the prince but Don Pedro, echoed by his brother, Don John, confirms Claudio's accusation. Claudio interrogates Hero about the man he saw at her window the night before. Hero denies the encounter. Claudio vows to love no more. Leonato seeks to be killed. Hero swoons. Don John, Don Pedro, and Claudio storm out of the church. Leonato, unable to believe that the two princes and Claudio could lie, accepts the slander as true and declares that if Hero is not dead he will kill her himself, disowning her. After Friar Francis recognizes her innocence and Benedick intuits that Don Pedro and Claudio have been misled by Don John, the good father directs Leonato to hide Hero away, to announce that she died upon being accused and to hold public mourning for her to change slander to remorse and to soften the heart of Claudio.

Beatrice and Benedick, suddenly alone before the altar, confess their love for one another. Benedick bids her to ask him to do anything for her. Beatrice answers with the chilling request, "[k]ill Claudio." Benedick asks Beatrice if she believes in her soul that Claudio wronged Hero. Receiving her affirmative answer, he agrees to challenge his friend and comrade-in-arms, Claudio.

Analysis

Shakespeare breaks the tone and movement of the comic action with a solemn ritual of marriage held before the altar, the visual effect of which is powerful and lends dignity to the scene. The first 21 lines of this scene are in prose, then in verse that ends in a quatrain (at 253) when the prose resumes.

Here we reach the climax of the many references to appearances and reality, when Claudio, locked in a world of sense evidence, in a church, before a congregation, accuses and refuses Hero, comparing her to a rotten orange. Dramatically, this crisis scene can be nothing but shocking, no matter how much we are prepared for it, and our mood is instantly altered.

Claudio, enjoying his revenge, takes his time to reject Hero and plays the injured lover to the hilt. He focuses his rejection on her name, asking her only one question (page 49):

Claudio: Let me but move one question to your
           daughter;
           And by that fatherly and kindly power
           That you have in her, bid her answer truly.

Leonato: I charge thee do so, as thou art my child.

Hero: O, God defend me! how am I beset!
           What kind of catechising call you this?

Claudio: To make you answer truly to your name.

Hero: Is it not Hero? Who can blot that name
           With any just reproach?

He can only justify his action with the words, "Are our eyes our own?" (page 49), echoed by Don Pedro, "Myself, my brother, and this grieved count/Did see her, did hear her" (page 49). Then Claudio tearfully teeters in antithesis and pummels Hero with paradoxes (page 50):

> Oh Hero, what a Hero hadst thou been,
> If half thy outward graces had been placed
> About thy thoughts and counsels of they heart!
> But fare thee well, most foul, most fair! farewell,
> Thou pure impiety and impious purity!

before storming out of the church, with a melodramatic vow never to love again, his immaturity revealed by his love for Hero's chaste image rather than her person.

When shocked Hero swoons, escaping into a coma, before an amazed congregation, her father, infected by the slander and burning with shame, falls into the cruel abyss of courtly code and seeks to regain his dignity with the death of his own daughter (page 50):

> Wherefore! Why doth not every earthly thing
> Cry shame upon her? Could she here deny
> The story that is printed in her blood?
> Do not live, Hero, do not ope thine eyes;
> For, did I think thou wouldst not quickly die,
> Thought I thy spirits were stronger than thy shames,
> Myself would, on the rearward of reproaches,
> Strike at thy life.

He lapses into self-pity; he cannot believe the princes could lie. Only the friar, Benedick, and Beatrice show any concern for Hero, the real victim. Beatrice instantly recognizes Hero's innocence and her eight words, "O, on my soul my cousin is belied!," prepare us for the dialogue she will have with Benedick at the end of this scene.

The friar's innate wisdom and long experience in dealing with his flock gives him another point of view (pages 51–52):

> Hear me a little;
> For I have only been silent so long,
> And given way unto this course of fortune,
> By noting of the lady: I have marked

> A thousand blushing apparitions
> To start into her face; a thousand innocent shames
> In angel whiteness beat away those blushes;
> And in her eye there hath appear'd a fire
> To burn the errors that these princes hold
> Against her maiden truth. Call me a fool;
> Trust not my reading nor my observations,
> Which with experimental seal doth warrant
> The tenor of my book; trust not my age.
> My reverance, calling, nor divinity,
> If this sweet lady lie not guiltless here
> Under some biting error.

Leonato cannot accept this readily since, holding to courtly code, he is ready to destroy whoever harmed him. Benedick astutely recognizes the error to be the practice of John, the Bastard. The benign hoax Father Francis suggests gives Leonato an immediate means of saving face and the experimental medicine he suggests for Claudio is guilt. We, the audience, look forward to seeing his remorse paraded before us.

The scene becomes poignant as everyone leaves the church except Benedick and Beatrice, still weeping for her cousin. The other characters have been exposed and we've been waiting for about a half-hour of playing time since Benedick and Beatrice recognized they were in love for this private moment. This is the climactic scene in the play when Benedick and Beatrice first confess their love for each other. Shakespeare used suspense and careful timing to bring us here and the rejection of Hero prepared us emotionally for its intimacy and intensity. Their crisis will counterpoint the one we have just witnessed and completely polarize the two plots. This is the point of greatest intensity in the play.

Benedick is the first to break through the wit-defended reserve that has kept them apart (page 54):

Benedick: I do love nothing in the world so well as you: Is
            not that strange?

Beatrice: As strange as the thing I know not. It were as
            possible for me to say I loved nothing so well

> as you: but believe me not; and yet I lie not. I
> confess nothing, nor I deny nothing. I am sorry
> for my cousin.

He renews his avowal of love and Beatrice answers, "I love you with so much of my heart that none is left to protest." Then he makes his fatal error:

Benedick: Come, bid me do anything for thee.
Beatrice: Kill Claudio.

The comedic element of the play, subdued until this moment, momentarily pops back into place when Benedick, who offered to do anything that Beatrice wanted, refuses the very first thing she asks. But Beatrice cannot be happy in her love until her kinswoman is vindicated, and she displays the full depth and range of her emotional landscape to Benedick. In that context, this terse dialogue takes place:

Benedick: Think you in your soul the Count Claudio hath
            wronged Hero?
Beatrice: Yea, as sure as I have a thought or a soul

Benedick is engaged and leaves to seek out Claudio. He has passed his first test, which is to choose between his love for Beatrice and his friendship for Claudio.

Benedick and Beatrice's meeting, originally designed to furnish sport for their superficial friends, has occurred in a context of crisis and suffering. Their direct speech has reached the level of sincerity and they alone have resisted Don John's evil and agreed to vindicate Hero.

Study Questions

1. How does Claudio reject Hero?

2. What does Don Pedro call Hero?

3. What fate does Leonato wish upon his daughter, Hero, after she swoons away? And what extreme measure is he willing to take to bring it about?

4. Did Beatrice sleep with Hero the night before?

5. Who declares his belief that Hero is innocent?

6. Whom does Benedick intuit as the author of the slander?

7. What does Friar Francis direct Leonato to do?

8. For whom does Beatrice weep?

9. Who confess their love for each other?

10. Who will Benedick challenge?

Answers

1. Claudio rejects Hero contemptuously as a wanton.

2. Don Pedro calls Hero a common stale.

3. Leonato wishes his daughter dead and he is willing to kill her himself.

4. No, Beatrice did not sleep with Hero the night before.

5. Friar Francis declares his belief that Hero is innocent.

6. Benedick intuits Don John as the author of the slander.

7. Friar Francis directs Leonato to hide Hero away, to announce that she died upon being accused, and to hold public mourning for her.

8. Beatrice weeps for her cousin, Hero.

9. Beatrice and Benedick confess their love for each other.

10. Benedick will challenge his friend, Claudio.

Suggested Essay Topics

1. Claudio and Don Pedro have publicly shamed Hero. Discuss the impact of this serious action on Hero and her kinsmen. Do you think they will ever forgive Claudio and Don Pedro? Cite specific dialogue from the text to support your position.

2. How does Leonato respond to the slander? What does his response tell you about his character? Why is he so easily swayed by the opinions of others? What do you suppose his next action will be? Why?

3. What is the wisdom of the priest? What faculty does he employ to see Hero's innocence? What kind of knowledge is the basis of his plan? Do you think his strategy will work? Cite the text to explain.

4. What moves Benedick to challenge Claudio? Do you think that Beatrice was right to ask him to kill Claudio? Defend your position.

Act IV, Scene II (pages 56–58)

New Character:

Sexton (Francis Seacole): *town clerk, a learned writer who, taking down the examination of Borachio and Conrade, recognizes the importance of its contents and immediately delivers it to Leonato*

Summary

This scene takes place at the jail. Dogberry, under the direction of the sexton, examines Borachio and Conrade. Speaking directly into Borachio's ear, Dogberry accuses him and Conrade of false knavery, which Borachio denies. The first watch and Seacole testify that they heard Borachio confess to receiving a thousand ducats from Don John for slandering Hero. The sexton announces that Don John fled after Hero was accused and refused and that Hero, upon the grief of this, suddenly died. He directs the constable to bind the men and bring them to Leonato's and leaves immediately to show the examination to the governor. About to be bound, Conrade calls Dogberry an ass. Scandalized, Dogberry wants all to remember that he is an ass, although it will not be written down.

Analysis

It is part of Shakespeare's genius to let the action of this play begin its fall with a new comic vision. Considered one of "the funniest scenes ever written" (Joseph Papp), this is where the final block of the play's action, which will resolve the polarized plots, begins.

Dogberry's opening line is, "Is our whole dissembly appeared?" We can imagine that he wears his very best judicial gown. Formal, saturnine, Conrade is immediately annoyed by him, presumably for being addressed as "sirrah", a contemptuous extension of sire, used to address inferiors. Dogberry's swearing–in ceremony would panic any lawyer:

Dogberry: Masters, do you serve God?

Conrade: ⎫
           ⎬ Yea, sir, we hope.
Borachio: ⎭

Dogberry: Write down, that they hope they serve God: and
            write God first; for God defend but God should
            go before such villains!

Fortunately, the sexton understands judicial procedure and moves the examination along by having the watch called as the accusers. This doesn't stop Dogberry's tangents and he keeps close watch that each word elicited is written down. As he hears the testimony of Seacole, seemingly for the first time (which would explain why he didn't know the importance of his prisoners when he spoke to Leonato), he tells the villains, "Thou wilt be condemned into everlasting redemption for this." The sexton confirms the events the watch testified to and leaves immediately to bring the examination to Leonato. Timing is still important to the action and Leonato must be prepared to move promptly.

As Dogberry is about "to opinion" them (translation: tie up), Conrade calls him a coxcomb and he is shocked at this stab to his office. But when Conrade calls him an ass, our petit bourgeois clown is beside himself, and his world of big words collapses (page 58):

I am a wise fellow; and, which is more, an officer; and,
which is more, a householder; and, which is more, as
pretty a piece of flesh as any is in Messina; and one that
knows the law, go to; and a rich fellow enough, go to;
and a fellow that hath had losses; and one that hath two
gowns and every thing handsome about him. Bring him
away. O, that I had been writ down an ass!

He parodies the "much ado" of the other characters in his self-important concern for the outward trappings of status and in his inability to grasp a clear thought.

Study Questions

1. Who is provided with a stool and a cushion?
2. Is Dogberry's examination of the prisoners direct and to the point?
3. Who moves the examination along and keeps it on point?
4. What does Dogberry whisper into Borachio's ear?
5. What is the testimony of the watch?
6. What is Dogberry's response upon hearing the watch testify that Count Claudio intended to accuse and refuse Hero?
7. Who confirms the testimony of the watch?
8. Who leaves to show Leonato the examination?
9. Does the news of Hero's death upon wrongful accusation have any effect on Conrade?
10. What does Dogberry want everyone to remember?

Answers

1. The sexton is provided with a stool and a cushion.
2. No. Dogberry's examination is extremely tangential and practically pointless.
3. The sexton moves the examination along and keeps it on point.
4. Dogberry whispers into Borachio's ear that "it is thought that you are false knaves."
5. The watch testifies that they heard Borachio call Don John a villain, who paid him a thousand ducats for slandering Hero and state that Count Claudio would disgrace and refuse Hero.

6. Upon hearing of Count Claudio's intention to accuse and refuse Hero, Dogberry tells Borachio that he will "be condemned into everlasting redemption for this."

7. The sexton confirms the testimony of the watch.

8. The sexton leaves to show Leonato the examination.

9. The news of Hero's death upon wrongful accusation has no effect on Conrade. On the contrary, it sobers him not at all, and he calls Dogberry an ass.

10. Dogberry wants everyone to remember that he is an ass.

Suggested Essay Topics

1. Why did Shakespeare put this broad comic scene directly after the crisis? What effect does this have on the audience? In what way does it move the action of the play forward? Explain.

2. Do you think this is the first time that Dogberry has examined a prisoner? Why is Dogberry unable to keep to the point? What is his mind preoccupied with? What would this examination have been like, had the sexton not intervened? What is Shakespeare telling us about the constabulatory of his time and their use of the legal system?

3. What prompts Conrade to call Dogberry an ass? Why does Dogberry perserve about being called an ass? Is he an ass? Cite passages from the text to defend your position.

SECTION SIX

Act V

Act V, Scene I (page 59–68)

Summary

The scene takes place in the street before the house of Leonato. Antonio tries to philosophize his brother, Leonato, out of his grief. Leonato says that his passion cannot be patched with proverbs and bids him to cease his counsel. Antonio advises him to make those who have harmed him suffer also, and Leonato vows to defend Hero's honor. At this point Claudio and Don Pedro cross their path. Both Leonato and Antonio challenge Claudio for the villainy of slandering Hero to death. Don Pedro tells them the charge against Hero was full of proof and refuses to listen further. Vowing that he will be heard, Leonato exits with his brother just as Benedick arrives.

Claudio and Don Pedro seek Benedick's wit to lift their spirits. Benedick challenges Claudio. Taking it as a jest, both Claudio and Don Pedro seek to enjoy their usual banter. Benedick tells Don Pedro that he must discontinue his company and repeats his challenge to Claudio. He informs them that Don John has fled Messina and that they killed an innocent lady. As Benedick exits, they realize that he is earnest. Don Pedro, in growing awareness, notes that his brother has fled.

The constables and the watch enter with Borachio and Conrade. Don Pedro recognizes them as his brother's men and asks Dogberry the nature of their offense. Finding Dogberry's answer too oblique to be understood, he questions Borachio. Borachio asks Don Pedro to let Count Claudio kill him and tells him that the watch overheard him confess his paid collusion in Don John's slander of Hero. Claudio now sees Hero in the light of the innocence he first loved her for.

Leonato and Antonio return with the sexton. Borachio declares sole responsibility for the death of Hero, but Leonato tells him that Don John, Don Pedro, and Claudio had a hand in it. Both Claudio and Don Pedro ask for a penance, claiming mistaking as their only sin. As penance, Leonato assigns them both the task of publicly mourning Hero and declaring her innocence. He assigns Claudio the further task of accepting his niece, sight unseen, in marriage the next morning. Dogberry takes this opportunity to tell Leonato that Conrade called him an ass and that the watch overheard the prisoners talk of another knave, one *Deformed*. Leonato thanks the watch and tips Dogberry. A thankful Dogberry humbly gives him leave to depart. As they leave, Don Pedro and Claudio promise to perform their penance. Leonato instructs the watch to bring the prisoners, then departs to question Margaret about her acquaintance with Borachio.

Analysis

Throughout the play Shakespeare has kept us informed of the truth while his characters deceive each other (at this point the sexton is on his way to Leonato's and Hero is not dead), which puts us into a somewhat removed orientation that increases the comic value of the action. In a sense, he has manipulated us into believing we're above it all. This scene opens with a grief–stricken but wordy Leonato, speaking in verse. Were his dialogue in a tragedy, we might be teary, but knowing that he will soon have proof that his daughter was slandered we are unlikely to extend him much sympathy, which tones down his indignation to a subtly comic level. Leonato refuses to be consoled by Antonio, dismissing him with (page 60):

> I pray thee, peace. I will be flesh and blood;
> For there was never yet philosopher
> That could endure the toothache patiently,

This echoes Benedick's toothache speech in Act III. He will take Antonio's suggestion to seek revenge, and he gets his opportunity immediately as Don Pedro and Claudio enter. The comedy leaps forward as Antonio flaunts his courage as he joins Leonato in challenging the young swordsman, knowing full well that neither Claudio nor the prince can dishonor themselves by fighting men of their advanced age. Don Pedro breaks up the mock challenge by saying a sympathetic word to Leonato, but when Don Pedro turns a cold ear to Leonato's appeal, he leaves, determined to be heard. His brother, Antonio, gives the exit a comic flourish by insinuating another challenge to come, a kind of or else. We, the audience, know all will be reconciled when Dogberry arrives. Note the dialogue change to prose at line 110, which continues until Dogberry's entrance, when it changes to a mixture of verse and prose.

Benedick enters and we know his mind; he is in his steely fighting mode. But his friends, Claudio and Don Pedro, who were seeking out his wit to lift their exhausted spirits (isolated by the renunciation) when they came across Leonato, don't get it. They take Benedick's dignified and sober expression as a joke, a masquerade to amuse them. This forces Benedick's attempts to deliver the challenge to Claudio to escalate the comedy somewhat as he takes him aside to deliver it. Claudio hears it but again doesn't understand it, and Don Pedro attempts to rag him about Beatrice. Benedick, void of levity, is firm and gentlemanly as he departs (page 64):

> My Lord, for your many courtesies I thank you; I must
> discontinue your company: your brother the bastard is
> fled from Messina: you have among you killed a sweet
> and innocent lady. For my Lord Lackbeard there, he and
> I shall meet, and till then peace be with him.

Now they know that he is earnest. And Don Pedro, in growing awareness, says, "Did he not say, my brother was fled?" which is the cue for Dogberry's entrance.

The theatrical spectacle of Dogberry and Verges parading their bound prisoners, secured by the watch, will get their attention, and Don Pedro immediately recognizes his brother's men.

Much Ado About Nothing

Of course, we know what is likely to happen when he inquires after their offense, and Dogberry does not disappoint us (pages 64–65):

> Marry, sir, they have committed false report;
> moreover, they have spoken untruths; secondarily,
> they are slanders; sixth and lastly, they have belied a
> lady; thirdly, they have verified unjust things; and to
> conclude, they are lying knaves.

The obliqueness of his answer allows them a short interlude of amusement until they find out the truth from Borachio (page 65):

> What your wisdoms could not discover, these
> shallow fools have brought to light; who, in the
> night, overheard me confessing to this man, how
> Don John your brother incensed me to slander the
> Lady Hero; how you were brought into the orchard;
> and saw me court Margaret in Hero's garments: how
> you disgraced her; when you should marry her.

There is an immediate tonal change. That Borachio was so converted by news of Hero's death implies that his drunken confession in Act III was a move in conscience. Friar Francis' curative has taken hold and to Claudio's eyes returns the pristine image of the Hero he wanted to marry. Claudio owns the sin of mistaking (sin means error, mistake, wander or stray, and in Hebrew means muddy). Dogberry reminds his men to specify that he is an ass. The scene, from Borachio's statement to this point reflects the passage of St. Paul in *I Corinthians*, 1:27–28:

> God hath chosen the foolish things of the world to
> confound the wise; and God hath chosen the weak
> things of the world to confound the things which are
> mighty; and base things of the world and things which
> are despised, hath God chosen, yea, and things which
> are not, to bring to nought things that are.

This may be the source for the invention of the constable and his watch. Certainly, Dogberry's discovery is purely providential, perhaps the answer to Friar Francis' prayer.

Now Shakespeare brings Leonato and Antonio back, and full of dignity, Leonato asks, "[w]hich is the villain?" When Borachio comes forth to claim full responsibility, Leonato, as he promised in his exit earlier in the scene, is heard (page 66):

> No, not so, villain; thou beliest thyself:
> Here stand a pair of honorable men;
> A third is fled; that had a hand in it.
> I thank you, princes, for my daughter's death:
> Record it with your high and worthy deeds:
> 'Twas bravely done, if you bethink you of it.

Claudio is instantly positioned to ask for a penance, echoed by Don Pedro. Leonato's wisdom, which he must have to be in the position of governor now shows through as he assigns the comic penance of hanging up verses at the empty tomb in a public mourning and the practical penance of clearing Hero's name. But the real test of Claudio's repentance is his willingness to marry Leonato's fictional niece, sight unseen.

Borachio's vindication of Margaret is necessary to keep the action from swerving out of its steady course to the resolution. This is Dogberry's opportunity to tag on his tangential thoughts with (page 67):

> Moreover, sir, which indeed is not under white and
> black, this plaintiff here, the offender, did call me
> an ass: I beseech you, let it be remembered in his
> punishment.

He goes on to share his concern with another *vagrom*, one *Deformed*, about whom he has apparently gathered an extended dossier, again parodying the much ado of the play's plot structure which was just as unreal, before saying adieu to Leonato:

> I humbly give you leave to depart; and if a merry
> meeting may be wished, God prohibit it!

Study Questions

1. What kind of philosopher does Leonato say never existed?

2. Which characters challenge Claudio?

3. What is Benedick's reply when asked by Claudio if he will use his wit?

4. What does Benedick tell Claudio and Don Pedro about Don John?

5. What does Borachio tell Don Pedro about the watch?

6. Does Leonato accept Borachio's claim to be solely responsible for Hero's death?

7. Does Borachio name Margaret as a co–conspirator in the slander of Hero?

8. What penance does Leonato give to Claudio and Don Pedro?

9. What does Dogberry want Leonato to remember when punishing Conrade?

10. Whom will Leonato talk with and why?

Answers

1. Leonato says, "[t]here was never yet a philosopher that could endure the toothache patiently."

2. Claudio is challenged by Leonato, by Antonio, and by Benedick.

3. Benedick replies, "It is in my scabbard. Shall I draw it?"

4. Benedick tells Claudio and Don Pedro that Don John has fled Messina.

5. Borachio tells Don Pedro "[w]hat your wisdoms could not discover, these shallow fools have brought to light."

6. No. Leonato tells Borachio that Don Pedro, Claudio, and Don John had a hand in it.

7. No. Borachio declares Margaret innocent of any conspiracy in the slander of Hero.

8. As penance, Leonato assigns them the task of informing Messina of Hero's innocence. Claudio will hang an epitaph upon her tomb, sing it to her bones that evening, and marry Leonato's niece, sight unseen, the next morning.

9. Dogberry wants Leonato to remember, when punishing Conrade, that he called him an ass.

10. Leonato will talk with Margaret to find out how her acquaintance grew with Borachio.

Suggested Essay Topics

1. Why do Don Pedro and Claudio seek Benedick to cheer them? Does their jocularity seem strange in light of the fact that they know Hero is dead? Why did they assume that Benedick was jesting? What did it take to sober them to the point of feeling anything for Leonato and Hero? What are they willing to own up to? What does this tell you about their characters? Use their dialogue to explain.

2. Borachio wishes to be killed for his villainy. Does this surprise you? Why does he protect Margaret and claim sole responsibility for killing Hero? What do these acts tell you about his character, and how did the action of the drama affect him? Interpret and explain.

3. For the penance requested by Claudio and Don Pedro, Leonato assigns them both the task of publicly mourning Hero and declaring her innocence. He assigns Claudio the further task of accepting his niece, sight unseen, in marriage. What wisdom does Leonato show in the assignment? Is it fair? What effect do you expect the performed penance to have on Claudio, Don Pedro, and the public? Give a detailed explanation.

Act V, Scene II (pages 68–70)

Summary

Benedick and Margaret meet outside Leonato's house. He bids her to call Beatrice to him and unsuccessfully attempts a sonnet. Beatrice complies with his request immediately. When Benedick toyfully marks (notes) that she comes when bidden, she bids him to tell her what has passed between he and Claudio. Benedick reports that Claudio undergoes his challenge. A witty interchange ensues as each seeks the other to tell the virtues for which they are loved and concludes with Benedick's declaration that they are "too wise to woo peaceably." Ursula appears to call them to Leonato's, with the news that Hero has been cleared, Don Pedro and Claudio were absolved, and Don John declared the villain.

Analysis

The double entendres between Benedick and Margaret that open this short prose scene serve to entertain us. This charming scene is technically important as part of the falling action of the play and prepares us for its solution and denouement as we await the findings of Leonato's judicial examination. This is Benedick's first breath of air since the chapel scene earlier in the morning, and his first opportunity to bask in the knowledge that his love for Beatrice is requited. He sings, no matter how pitifully, William Elderton's ditty, "The God of love/That sits above/And knows me/And knows me," which is sure to draw a chuckle from the audience as he attempts sonnet-writing and concludes (pages 68–69):

> in loving, Leander the good swimmer, Troilus the
> first employer of panders, and a whole bookful of
> these quondam carpet-mongers, whose names yet
> run smoothly in the even road of a blank verse, why,
> they were never so truly turned over and over as
> my poor self in love.... No, I was not born under a
> rhyming planet, nor I cannot woo in festival terms.

Beatrice's entrance saves him from the attempt. His short experiment with institutionalized romance completed, he will love Beatrice honestly and in his own way.

It is obvious that he is more interested in wooing Beatrice than talking about his challenge to Claudio. As their good–natured dialogue continues in explorations of nimble wit, Benedick observes, "Thou and I are too wise to woo peaceably."

Study Questions

1. Who does Benedick meet at the opening of the scene?

2. Was Benedict born under a rhyming planet?

3. Does Beatrice come when she is called by Benedick?

4. What news did Beatrice want to find out?

5. What does Benedick tell Beatrice about Claudio?

6. For which of Benedick's bad parts did Beatrice first fall in love with him?

7. Why does Benedick suffer love for Beatrice?

8. Why can't Benedick and Beatrice woo peaceably?

9. Who is Don Worm?

10. What news does Ursula bring?

Answers

1. Benedick meets Margaret at the opening of the scene.

2. Benedick was not born under a rhyming planet.

3. Beatrice comes when she is called by Benedick.

4. Beatrice wanted to find out if Benedick challenged Claudio.

5. Benedick tells Beatrice that Claudio undergoes his challenge.

6. Beatrice first fell in love with Benedick for all of his bad parts.

7. Benedick suffers love for Beatrice because he loves her against his will.

8. Benedick and Beatrice are too wise to woo peaceably.

9. Don Worm is the action of the conscience, traditionally described as the gnawing of a worm.

10. Ursula brings the news that "It has been proved my Lady Hero hath been falsely accused, the Prince and Claudio mightily abused, and Don John is the author of all, who is fled and gone."

Suggested Essay Topics

1. What does Benedick mean when he tells us he was not born under a rhyming planet? What does he mean when he says he cannot woo in festival terms? Does this mean he is a bad lover? How do you think he will love Beatrice? Explain.

2. Benedick tells Beatrice that they are too wise to woo peaceably. Is this true? Do you think less wise people woo any more peaceably than they do? Explain, citing examples from the text.

Act V, Scene III (pages 70–71)

Summary

Claudio and Don Pedro, accompanied by a party of lords and musicians, arrive at the monument of Leonato to perform a public mourning for Hero. Claudio reads an epitaph which declares her innocence and then hangs it up at her tomb. Balthasar sings a hymn to Diana, patroness of chastity, entreating her to forgive Hero's slanderers. Claudio vows to do the rite yearly. At dawn the mourners leave, each going their separate way. Claudio and Don Pedro will change their garments and go to Leonato's for the wedding.

Analysis

The redemption scene, with its epitaph, song, and dialogue, is wholly in rhyme with the exception of the first two lines. At midnight our penitents arrive at Leonato's monument and withdraw into a world of contrition as they enter the damp tomb to experience the spiritual medicine of Friar Francis' restorative, accompanied by a silent black-robed procession with flickering tapers.

Claudio reads the epitaph to Hero, "done to death by slanderous tongues," that he has written (which requires deep-felt delivery to work), hangs up the scroll for public scrutiny, and calls for the dirge (page 71):

> Pardon, goddess of the night,
> Those that slew thy virgin knight;
> For the which, with songs of woe,
> Round about her tomb they go.
>> Midnight, assist our moan;
>> Help us to sigh and groan,
>>> Heavily, heavily:
>> Graves, yawn and yield your dead,
>> Till death be uttered,
>>> Heavily, heavily.

While it is sung the mourners circle the tomb. The tone is solemn. They beg pardon of Diana, moon goddess and patroness of chastity, and invoke midnight and the shades of the dead to assist them as they proclaim Hero's innocent death.

This scene carries an other-worldly quality and its comic element is subdued almost entirely, asking for no more than a knowing chuckle. We are convinced that Friar Francis' nostrum has taken hold when Claudio volunteers to perform the ceremony yearly, until his death, and his reformation prepares the audience to accept him as a worthy husband for Hero.

Study Questions

1. Where does the action take place?

2. What is the action?

3. Who reads the epitaph to Hero?

4. After reading the epitaph, what does Claudio do with the scroll?

5. Who sings the hymn to Hero?

6. Who is the goddess of the night?

7. How often does Claudio vow to perform this rite?

8. At what time of day do they end their rite?

9. Who dismisses the mourning company?

10. What will Claudio and Don Pedro do next?

Answers

1. The action takes place at the tomb of Hero, in the monument of Leonato.

2. The action is a public rite of mourning.

3. Claudio reads the epitaph to Hero.

4. After reading the epitaph, Claudio hangs up the scroll.

5. Balthasar sings the hymn to Hero.

6. Diana, the moon goddess and patroness of chastity, is the goddess of the night.

7. Claudio vows to do this rite yearly.

8. They end their rite at dawn.

9. Don Pedro dismisses the mourning company.

10. Claudio and Don Pedro will change their clothes and proceed to Leonato's.

Suggested Essay Topics

1. Claudio vows to perform this rite of mourning to Hero yearly. Does this vow indicate a change in consciousness? Explain the rite of passage Claudio has gone through while performing his penance, detailing each inner action of conscience as you see it in your mind's eye.

2. Why does Shakespeare place this action during the night in a tomb, lit only by candles, and end it at the break of dawn? What does this symbolize? What theatrical effect does this have on the audience? Would this scene, though a public mourning, have worked as well in full sunlight? Explain.

Act V, Scene IV (pages 72–75)

Summary

This scene takes place in the hall in Leonato's house. Musicians are seated in the gallery. Hero, the prince, and Claudio have been declared innocent, and Margaret in some fault for the slander. Benedick is relieved that he need no longer keep Claudio under his challenge. Leonato directs Hero and the other ladies to withdraw and return, masked, when he sends for them. He directs Antonio to play the father of the bride. When Benedick asks Leonato for Beatrice's hand in marriage and Leonato exposes the double gull, Benedick, though nonplussed at Leonato's answer, reaffirms his request and receives Leonato's blessing.

Prince Don Pedro and Claudio arrive with attendants. Claudio answers in the affirmative when asked by Leonato if he will marry his niece. While Antonio summons Hero and the ladies, Claudio attempts to tease Benedick. Benedick briskly dismisses Claudio with an insult to his heritage. Antonio returns with Hero and the ladies, who are masked. Claudio swears before the friar that he will marry Antonio's masked daughter. When Hero lifts her veil, he and Don Pedro are amazed. Leonato explains that she was dead only as long as her slander lived, which the friar promises to explain. Benedick asks the friar which of the ladies is Beatrice. Unmasking, she coyly steps forth from the line of women. Benedick asks Beatrice if she loves him and she responds "no more than reason," which he echoes, and when Beatrice asks Benedick if he loves her, they both detail the particulars of their separate gulls, at which point Claudio and Hero step forth with papers, written in their hands, which evidence their love for each other. Benedick stops the wordplay with a kiss. When Don Pedro attempts to mock Benedick as a married man, Benedick refuses the bait and declares that since he purposes to marry he will not entertain any thing against it, including his own past parodies of the state. Claudio and Benedick resume their friendship. Benedick spiritedly calls for music and dance to lighten their hearts and advises the matchmaker, Don Pedro, to "get thee a wife, get thee a wife." A messenger arrives with news that Don John has been taken, and is being brought back to Messina. The play ends with Benedick's call to the pipers and an exuberant dance.

Analysis

In the denouement and resolution of the play, Shakespeare ties its loose ends up amiably, rejoining the polarized plots with a reconciliation scene. He clearly indicates he will do this in Friar

Francis' dialogue, "Well I'm glad that all things sorts so well." He immediately tells us that the prince and Claudio have been absolved, that Margaret underwent Leonato's examination and escaped with slight censure, and that Benedick has released Claudio from his challenge. The first 90 lines of this scene are in verse, including speeches by Benedick and Beatrice, and the rest is in prose except for the messenger's two verse lines interjected at its end.

Leonato's confession of the double gull does not sway Benedick from his determination to marry Beatrice. Although he tells Leonato that his answer is "enigmatical," it is unlikely that anyone as alert as Benedick does not understand his meaning, and his comical remark serves not only to end any exploration of the matter at this time and to affirm his commitment, but also serves to advise us that Benedick has reached a new level of self-acceptance.

Both Leonato and Benedick continue their reserve with Don Pedro and Claudio until the penance is fulfilled and their dialogue is direct, shorn of ornamentation. Benedick ignores the prince's gibe about his "February face" and disposes of Claudio's crude rally with caustic severity. Claudio's insensitivity (basically a play for masculine approval and probably developed during the war), though he is well-bred, indicates the immaturity which caught him in the circumstances of the play to begin with. The inappropriateness of his remarks serve to maintain a comic element to counterpoint the other characters' reserve. Without it, the denouement of the play would flatten.

Claudio, having submitted all choice to Leonato, has mourned at the tomb and, having rejected Hero on the basis of outer appearance (hubris), must now prove himself by accepting Leonato's masked niece as his wife (nemesis). His submission assures Leonato that there will be no similar trouble in the family in the future. It is here that Shakespeare puts his greatest emphasis on the mask motif and the row of masked ladies both parallel and counterpoint the masquerade ball in Act II, in which the men wore the masks.

Hero lifts her veil, after Claudio vowed before the holy friar to marry her, and we see an amazed Claudio. The benign hoax had such a salutary effect that his contrition makes it hard for him to believe that she is alive. Reunited with the reborn Hero, he is readily forgiven, in the Christian tradition, for, after all, the wrong done to Hero was not a betrayal of love and trust but an assault on her reputation and the break-off of a desirable marriage—wrongs easily righted. The decorous dialogue, so elaborate in the exposition, is now pared to the bone, void of polite routine. All oblique references are gone, and any question promises a prompt answer. At this point, the Claudio-Hero plot is resolved as the giving of trust and the move toward faith. The suspense has ended; they will be married.

Our three-dimensional players, Benedick and Beatrice, complete their journey that began as a trial of verbal supremacy, developed as the ability to see themselves as part of the human comedy rather than clever onlookers, and now concludes with the spontaneous and loving expression of their combined, generous wit. Their dialogue has lost none of its vitality and now expresses itself in unchecked joy and merriment that springs from their new levels of inner awareness.

Beatrice continues to keep Benedick wondering by playfully hiding herself among the masked ladies, secure in the knowledge that he will seek her out, and steps forward coyly when he asks where she is. They gracefully face the truth about their courtship publicly in an articulate exchange which is the exact antithesis that matchmaker Don Pedro had looked forward to:

> The sport will be, when they hold one an opinion
> of another's dotage, and no such matter: that's the
> scene I would like to see, which will be merely a
> dumbshow.

A renewed Benedick will be no man's fool when it comes to the subject of love, and he responds to Don Pedro's baiting question, "how dost thou, Benedick, the married man?" with:

> I'll tell thee what, prince; a college of wit-crackers
> cannot flout me out of my humour. Dost thou think

I care for a satire or an epigram? No: if a man will be
beaten with brains, a' shall wear nothing handsome
about him. In brief, since I do purpose to marry, I
will think nothing to any purpose that the world can
say against it; and therefore never flout at me for
what I have said against it; for man is a giddy thing,
and this is my conclusion.

So ends the fashion metaphor. Benedick is saying that a slave
to convention will never be true to himself; that if he lives in fear
of an epigram, he dare not marry a beautiful woman. He responds
to Claudio's macho baiting by declaring his friendship for him. All
defenses collapsed, Benedick insists on celebrating with music
and dance and tells Don Pedro, the matchmaker, to "get thee a
wife, get thee a wife."

This ends the play. Shakespeare has completed the three
phases of his play: recognition of love, stress of trial, and resolution with love's confirmation. The lesson the play teaches is
to learn to discriminate properly and to estimate everything at
its true value. In the end, the counterplots initiated by the two
princes have brought only the good result of strengthening love.
Perhaps Shakespeare is saying that all of us, as Claudio claims, sin
only through "mistaking".

It is not surprising that this is the only play of Shakespeare
that ends with a dance because a play of such musicality as *Much
Ado About Nothing* can only end with a dance—an exuberant
dance! We have taken the emotional journey with the players, and
renewed, we go our separate ways.

Study Questions

1. Who is declared innocent?

2. When Benedick asks Leonato for Beatrice's hand and
   Leonato reveals the double gull, what is Benedick's
   response?

3. Who is the masked lady that Claudio swore to marry and
   how does he respond when she unveils herself?

4. What paper does Claudio produce?

5. How does Benedick stop Beatrice's mouth?

6. What is Benedick's conclusion?

7. Who wants to dance and why?

8. What advice does Benedick give Don Pedro?

9. What news does the messenger bring?

10. Which plays of Shakespeare end with a dance?

Answers

1. Hero, the prince, and Claudio are declared innocent.

2. Benedick's response is, "[y]our answer, sir, is enigmatical."

3. Claudio is amazed to find the masked lady that he swore to marry is none other than Hero.

4. Claudio produces a paper containing a halting sonnet written by Benedick.

5. Benedick stops Beatrice's mouth with a kiss.

6. Benedick's conclusion is "man is a giddy thing."

7. Benedick wants to dance to lighten their hearts and their wive's heels.

8. Benedick advises Don Pedro to "[g]et thee a wife, get thee a wife."

9. The messenger brings the news that Don John is taken and will be brought back to Messina.

10. No other plays of Shakespeare end with a dance.

Suggested Essay Topics

1. Why does Hero readily forgive Claudio for accusing and refusing her? Do you think this is a typical reaction? What do you think their marriage will be like? Explain.

2. As Benedick's values change during the play, so do his musical allusions. In this scene, it is Benedick who wants music, and specifically, pipers—even before the wedding! What does this indicate to you? Citing specific passages, compare this scene with his previous responses to music

and discuss how they indicate his growing response to love.

3. Benedick tells Prince Don Pedro, the matchmaker, to get himself a wife. What kind of wife would he require? Would he invite his brother, Don John, to the wedding? Do you think he is ready for marriage? Why? Explain.

SECTION SEVEN

Bibliography

Barish, Jonas A. *Pattern and Purpose in the Prose of Much Ado About Nothing*. Rice University Studies, 60:2, 1974, pp. 19–30.

Berry, Ralph. *Much Ado About Nothing: Structure & Texture*. English Studies 52, 1971, pp. 211–223.

Fillmore, Charles. *Metaphysical Bible Dictionary*, Missouri: Unity, 1931.

Furness, Horace Howard, ed. *Much Ado About Nothing, A New Variorum Edition of Shakespeare*. New York: Dover Publications, Inc., 1964.

Gaskell, G.A. *Dictionary of all Scriptures and Myths*. New York: Julian Press, Inc., 1973.

Hockey, Dorothy C. *Notes Notes, Forsooth...*. Shakespeare Quarterly 8, 1957, pp. 353–358. Delineates the pattern of misnoting or false noting as the thematic device of the play.

Holy Bible, Philadelphia: National Bible Press, conformable to the edition of 1611 commonly known as the King James Version.

Owen, Charles A., Jr. *Comic Awareness, Style, and Dramatic Technique in Much Ado About Nothing*. Boston University Studies in English, Vol. 5, No. 4, Winter 1961, pp. 193–207.

Quiller–Couch, Sir Arthur and John Dover Wilson, ed. *Much Ado About Nothing, The Works of Shakespeare*. London: Cambridge University Press, 1969.

Shaw, George Bernard. *Our Theatres in the Nineties*. 3 vols. London: Constable & Co., Ltd., 1932.

Skeat, Rev. Walter W. *A Concise Etymological Dictionary of the English Language*. New York: Capricorn Books, 1963.

Stauffer, Donald A. *Shakespeare's World of Images*. New York: W.W. Norton and Company, Inc., 1949.

Stevenson, David L., ed. *Much Ado About Nothing*. New York: Signet, 1964.

Swinburne, Algernon Charles. *A Study of Shakespeare*. London 1880.

Wey, James J. *"To Grace Harmony": Musical Design in Much Ado About Nothing*. Boston University Studies in English, Vol. IV, No. 3, Autumn 1960, pp. 181–188.

DOVER·THRIFT·EDITIONS

PLAYS